VIRGIN
and Other Stories

APRIL AYERS LAWSON has been awarded the Plimpton Prize for Fiction, as well as a writing fellowship from The Corporation of Yaddo. Her fiction has appeared in *Granta, Oxford American,* and *Vice*, among other publications, and been anthologized in *The Unprofessionals: New American Writing from the Paris Review.* She has lectured in the Creative Writing Department at Emory University, and as the Kenan Visiting Writer at the University of North Carolina at Chapel Hill. *Virgin and Other Stories* is her first book.

VIRGIN

and Other Stories

APRIL AYERS LAWSON

GRANTA

Granta Publications, 12 Addison Avenue, London W11 4QR

First published in Great Britain by Granta Books as an ebook in 2016 and
in print in 2017
This paperback edition published in 2018

First published the USA in 2016 by Farrar, Straus and Giroux

Grateful acknowledgment is made to the following publications, in which these
stories originally appeared, in slightly different form: *Crazyhorse* ("The Way You
Must Play Always"); *Five Chapters* ("The Negative Effects of Homeschooling");
Oxford American ("Three Friends in a Hammock"); *The Paris Review* ("Virgin");
VICE (an excerpt from "Vulnerability," published as "Three Love Stories");
ZYZZYVA (an excerpt from "Vulnerability," published as "Vulnerability").

A CIP catalogue record for this book is available from the British Library.

1 3 5 7 9 10 8 6 4 2

ISBN 978 1 84708 561 0 (paperback)
ISBN 978 1 84708 562 7 (ebook)

Designed by Jo Anne Metsch

Offset by Avon DataSet Ltd, Bidford on Avon, B50 4JH

Printed and bound by CPI Group (UK) Ltd, Croydon, CR0 4YY

www.grantabooks.com

For my grandmother Francis Rothel,
whose favorite verse was
"For God hath not given us the spirit of fear; but of power,
and of love, and of a sound mind" (2 Timothy 1:7)

CONTENTS

VIRGIN

I

Jake hadn't meant to stare at her breasts, but there they were, absurdly beautiful, almost glowing above the plunging neckline of the faded blue dress. He'd read the press releases, of course. He recalled, from an article, her description of nursing her last child only six months before her first radiation treatment. Then he noticed she wasn't wearing a bra.

What did they have inside them: saline or silicone? And how did these feel, respectively? He probably stared too long. (But how could she expect people not to stare when she wore a dress cut like that?)

She'd noticed.

Had his wife noticed? Doubtful. She noticed so little about him these days.

"This is some place you have here," he said too quickly.

Though they weren't exactly friends, she'd come into his office before, with her little girl, and they'd talked about her plans to sponsor a mobile mammography unit. They'd formed a connection, it had seemed to him then, and their time together lingered taut as a problem in his mind. But now she'd definitely seen him staring at her breasts, about which she must have had extraordinarily complicated feelings, and she was annoyed.

"What does that mean exactly?"

"I just meant you have a nice home," Jake replied.

"It's too big, isn't it?"

He didn't know how to reply: the house, miles from the road and framed, on this spring evening, by an almost other-worldly lushness of green, was in fact an old plantation estate that included detached quarters for both servants and slaves; of course it was, technically, too big, but what could he say? "It's lovely," he managed.

Dissatisfied, she turned to his wife. "Wouldn't *you* say a house this size is way too big, even for a family of five?"

Sheila, surveying the foyer, tilting her heart-shaped face up toward the high, vast ceiling, seemed actually to be considering the question. Jake was mortified.

To his relief she replied that she was sure the children loved all the space.

"Actually my children seem to crave small spaces," the hostess said. "The twins once spent an entire day inside a packing crate. When I was their age I hated tight spaces. I screamed when people shut the door to my room, which I shared with my brother and was about the size of a closet. I'm afraid we're doomed to want the opposite of what we have." She looked back at Jake and seemed in that moment to forgive him. "Well, you two should go on in and have a drink. Don't you look adorable, like newlyweds!"

People often immediately identified them as newlyweds. Jake worried over this, but when he asked Sheila if it bothered her, she laughed. She said what it really meant was that people were thinking of the two of them having good sex. Sheila's implied understanding of the difference between good and bad sex also disturbed him. The problem with marrying a virgin, he realized now, was that you were marrying a girl who would become a woman only after the marriage.

"You can let go of my hand now," she said to him at the party that night.

He hadn't known he'd been holding it.

Sheila was twenty-two, and had just graduated with a degree in music from Bob Jones University. Jake was twenty-six and before this job had worked as a reporter at a daily newspaper in Charlotte. He had loved the stink of newsprint that clung to his cubicle and the late-night deadlines, the euphoria that came over him after filing a story. Then, at a party—she'd driven up to Charlotte with some friends—he'd met Sheila, shyly beautiful and somehow detached from the noise and flash of people in their twenties parading their allure. They'd been at the apartment of a friend of a friend. When he went out on the balcony to smoke, he'd found her sitting there in a lawn chair, in a robin's-egg-blue dress that glowed against the orange sunset, staring up at him with a sense of expectation so palpable he felt late. She had seemed to him, with her glossy auburn hair and knowing expression, unashamedly pure, and all of the warm summer night they'd sat out on the porch of the friend's apartment, watching people through the glass doors and making up comic bits of conversation for them, analyzing their gestures. He hadn't had dinner. Someone from a neighboring apartment was grilling meat and despite the smell of the steak, he stayed by her side.

"I hate flirting," she'd said at the point in the night when people were beginning to couple off. He followed her gaze into the living room of the apartment, at a girl striding across the room in stilettos. "And I hate high-heeled shoes." He'd noticed, when he came out onto the porch to smoke, the abandoned blue heels, her bare feet. "Do you know why people like them so much?" He said he had assumed it was because they were flattering to the leg, and she excitedly replied, "Lordosis. You know: the arch of a woman's back during copulation?" He watched as she slipped on her heels and told him to pay close attention to the effect they had on her posture. "Isn't our culture sick?" she said. He studied her ass, her toned calves, and agreed wholeheartedly while she continued with her criticisms, aware that she, cheeks flushed in the lamplight passing through the glass, was also aroused. She said that she wished he would stop smoking because she didn't want him to get cancer, and he promptly ground the cigarette he was smoking beneath his heel. She asked him to hand over the pack, and, staring right into his eyes, she tossed it behind her, over the railing. He didn't know whether to be irritated or impressed: she was so ethereal, but also kind of a bitch. By the time he made plans to drive the hour and a half to her town to see her the next weekend, he thought he might already be in love.

The wedding had taken place in a cathedral carved into the side of a mountain, at sunset, at the very end of summer. It was near-perfect, marred only by Sheila's family having to deal with the arrival of an estranged, drunken uncle—someone had promptly called him a cab before the ceremony—and by his mother arriving just as the quartet began the first piece, in the skirt and blouse she'd worn the evening before at the rehearsal dinner. He was quietly humiliated—he knew she'd driven down to Atlanta after dinner, to meet a man she'd been chatting with on the Internet—and annoyed by the lean look of her, her too-long, graying hair. He did not want to think of her growing old alone. But the tension faded the moment Sheila, in her ivory gown, shoulders bared, approached the altar. Though she moved toward him, he was stirred by the sensation that he was approaching her, and he felt none of the fear other married men had warned him about.

She had begun with the excuses five months ago. He'd be watching television, drinking a beer after work, when she'd come into the living room to announce that she needed to go out and buy some paper towels, or that she craved ice cream she'd failed to purchase the last time she went out. "Let me come with you," he'd say. But she'd argue that she wouldn't be long, that she had a new CD to listen to, and this meant she wanted to be by herself. Early on he'd realized she preferred listening to new music alone, because he was unmusical, or at least compared to her. And so he let her go. Sometimes she came back right away. But a few times she'd stayed gone for hours. On Thursdays she had a late orchestra practice, and after one of these sessions didn't come home until close to two in the morning, claiming she'd had coffee with a female friend from the orchestra and lost track of time. That evening, he'd pulled into the drive at the same time she was dashing across the walkway, and recalled that she'd looked especially nice for her practice, her usually straight hair in the waves she sometimes wore when they went out. After they embraced, she reached back for his hand, holding it thoughtfully in her own, her thumb reassuringly—too reassuringly—massaging his palm. "Skip it," he begged, testing her, but she seemed to look through him. She laughed as she turned toward her car.

————

One afternoon, meaning to call his wife at home, he'd heard his mother's voice speak; he'd accidentally dialed her number. He made small talk for a few minutes. But in asking what he thought of as harmless questions, he must have accidentally let some of the suspicion he felt for his wife leak into his voice, because his mother began to laugh at him. She said, "Aren't both of us a little old for you to be calling to check up on me?"

"Checking up" on her was what she used to call his less artful enquiries into her love life, the ones he made as a teenager.

"What did I say?" he asked her, already feeling a too-familiar sense of frustration.

"It's not what you say," she explained, exasperated with him in the manner of a daughter with her father. "It's your tone. You talk to me like you've already decided I'm going to tell you something you don't want to hear. Or like whatever I'm about to say to you is a lie."

Jake thought of her when she was in love—how, when he was small, she would bend down to peer with such intensity into his eyes before school, her hands reverentially skimming his hair and cheeks before coming to rest lightly, worshipfully, on his shoulders; how, outside, walking through the cool air toward the bus stop, he felt like a sacred being, warm with his mother's love and the wonder of his own light. He had been too young then to understand the effects of romance: that she spent on him the excess of her feelings for some man. In the lull between men she could never touch him in quite the same way. Now he sighed. When he hurt her he became to her every man who'd hurt her.

"What else?"

"I just hope you don't talk to your wife like you talk to me," she replied.

He wanted to trust his wife, he truly did. But he couldn't stop himself from noticing, in public, the way Sheila returned the types of male glances she'd before seemed not to notice. He'd be talking to her about some movie they'd just seen, or about work, and he would see her eyes dart away from him to study the back of a young waiter, or the shoulders of a man older than her father. Occasionally, he'd even seen his wife lock eyes with a stranger and offer this person a flirtatious half-smile—right in front of him—and when Jake asked if she knew that man, his way of telling her he'd caught her, she'd say, "He just reminded me of someone I used to know." Or, in a puzzled, dismissive tone, as if Jake were paranoid, "I'm just being friendly." It was upsetting not only in itself, but also because it was the kind of behavior he associated with his mother. Again he felt the unease he'd felt as a little boy, nervously cherishing the brief periods of peace they had between her lovers, all the while afraid that any of the strange men they encountered in shops, at the park, at the zoo or museum, could very well end up in their home. He understood how quickly their movie nights and pancake suppers, their reading the newspaper together on Saturday morning—her happily questioning him about what he'd read, delighting in his answers ("Why don't you help me wrap my mind around that, Mr. Know-it-all?"), would be replaced by the drama of her infatuation, by a monster (gross and strong and idiotic they seemed to him) who wished him dead.

Now, at this party, on this spring night, in this huge old house, one room giving way to another in mazelike fashion, all of them familiarly pleasant with their cleverly mismatched furniture and Oriental rugs, like décor from a magazine, he would have to mind Sheila. Or, he wouldn't be able to mind her. He already felt her wanting to slip away from him and explore, and knew that she would.

She was as usual oblivious to his suspicion. "That woman," Sheila said, grinning, speaking of their hostess, "is so interesting. I wonder if she was that strange before she was rich."

She wore a strapless dark blue dress. She kept rolling back her bare shoulders and stretching her arms. She seemed always to be stretching lately, especially in public.

"I doubt it," he said, deciding not to let on all he knew of her (as if he could've even *explained* what he knew). "Things like that change people."

"Do you really think people change, or just seem to change?" Sheila said, scanning the crowd. She would just as soon take the opposite position. She was like that. She never betrayed guilt about what she was doing to him, and that she behaved so normally around him made him think she either loved him so much that her feelings for other men didn't affect her feelings for him, or that she didn't love him at all. "Because I think everything is already there inside of you," she went on. "What you are. By the time childhood is over. What I think is that you just become this purer and purer version of what you already are."

"You mean *who* you already are."

"No. That's not what I meant," softly, thoughtfully, as if to herself.

II

He'd found out about her virginity on their third date, over pasta at an Italian restaurant, after the waiter handed them the wine list. "You know I should probably tell you now: I don't drink. Both sets of my grandparents were alcoholics and so no one in my family drinks. But I don't mind that you do. Also, I guess I should tell you, too, that I don't have sex. Until I get married. I mean, I'm a virgin. Sex isn't just a physical thing to me, but a deeply spiritual thing that I only want to experience with my future husband, to whom I want to offer my purity as a gift. Just don't want you to get the wrong idea."

He understood that she had made this little speech before, that she offered it as both a challenge and discouragement. But he was not discouraged. In that moment he had become hypnotized by the miracle of her mouth, her hands, her chest rising with her breath. He had thoughts he'd have been too embarrassed to ever speak aloud: waking to an untouched blanket of snow, freshly cut flowers, the smell of baking bread. He thought, strangely, of women emerging from the water of the local pool, wet hair heavy against their shoulders, rivulets of water cascading down bare limbs. In grade school, on picture day, he had seen the ivory hem of a girl's new dress on the playground splattered with mud.

He found himself adjusting the cuff of his sleeve, smoothing his hair.

"I respect that very much," he told her. Even the sight of her fork spearing food now intrigued him.

She hadn't acted surprised.

Pictures of Sheila as a child revealed a bespectacled, awkwardly thin person in baggy clothes. Her parents were devout fundamentalists whose black-and-white television stayed up in the attic, and they limited their library to biblical commentary. Friendly but guarded, they watched him with eyes he couldn't read. Wariness fringed their air of puritanical optimism, and their voices slipped into warning tones creepy to him when the sun had just gone down and the beige of their living room appeared gray before the turning on of lamps. But her mother's frequent offers of snacks and tea reassured him.

"People are born with an emptiness inside them," said her father, a big bearded man who worked in construction. While they talked, he gently, rhythmically stroked the matted back of the family's aged terrier, his hand as wide as the dog. "If you don't fill it with God, it grows. Emptiness begets emptiness," he said. "Nothing begets nothing."

"Love begets love," her mother said. She was a slender woman with a kind smile and dark, boyish haircut, her blouses a size too large.

"Love begets compassion," the father corrected. "And compassion begets love. Compassion is God's love." Sheila's mother nodded emphatically. Sheila was picking at her cuticles and looked up to glance over at him, rolled her eyes. (She was like this—sometimes regarding her religion seriously, sometimes speaking of it almost as a joke she went along with.)

"Do you believe in God's love?" her father asked Jake.

Of course, Jake said; though, *Of course not*, he thought. His mother had dabbled in every major faith and some of the minor ones, had even flirted with the occult, and religion seemed to him an unnecessary and too often desperate exhaustion of will. The self-infatuated tone of people's voices when they spoke of their intimacy with a higher power depressed him. He would force himself not to cringe when Sheila's mother, smelling of the same linen-scented detergent her daughter used, hugged him goodbye and whispered into his ear, "God loves you." And when, a month before the wedding—breath drawn, eyes shut—he allowed Sheila's father to drown him in the water of the baptistery at their little country church, he felt nauseated.

But he liked imagining Sheila, with her red hair and look of calm curiosity, emerging from this little cave of deprivation. In her college photos—in the succession of them, from freshman to senior year—you could see her, whom he thought of as his Sheila, distinguishing herself from this world. The cave became the background that defined her. Her body grew graceful, shoulders rolled back, hair longer and even a deeper auburn, and the simplicity of her clothes elegant; but what changed most was the way she reacted to the camera. The shy, averted gaze of the adolescent gave way to a head-on stare, her eyes lit with something like impatience. Her school uniform— the long khaki skirts and white button-down blouses—seemed to emphasize her ease in her body, an ease that communicated to him latent sexual appetite. She had, with her pouty lips, what he and his friends, as teenagers, would've happily referred to as "a slutty face," and the irony of this made him laugh.

He thought, he felt, that she couldn't wait to lose her virginity to him.

She seemed to communicate this through her long legs, bared by short skirts—she wore short skirts constantly now that she'd graduated from the school, except when they visited her parents, for whom she dressed like an elementary school librarian—and through the way she would press her breasts up against him when they kissed. When his hands became too insistent, she'd pull her face from his, her long red hair falling into his mouth, and say, in a sweet, apologetic voice, "We need to stop now." Disentangle herself from his arms. It was almost as if he were with a high school girl.

He didn't mind. Their future together had soon taken shape in his fantasies. She was pure and smart and talented—she played first viola in the county orchestra—and passionate. One evening, over the phone, she told him that when, after having just slid her bow across the strings for the first measure of the second piece in a concert, she felt the vibrations of all the other instruments in the air around her, she shivered with what she believed was orgasmic energy. The formality of her concerts became for him—from his seat among strangers in the dim auditorium, gazing up at Sheila in her black dress, in the circle of light she shared with the other players—a sort of erotic tease.

The first evening, in the hotel room, Sheila wore black-lace lingerie and kissed him enthusiastically; but as his hands and lips descended past her belly, she began to tense. She pushed his hand down, against her thigh. He tried again, and she finally pulled away from him, drawing the slightly stiff hotel sheets around her, complaining she felt sick from the plane. He knew she was scared—so much had happened: the ceremony, the flight, her first trip to London. (She'd wanted to hear the London Symphony.) They spent the rest of the night cuddling in the hotel bed and watching European movies that seemed to suggest people could never really comprehend their true realities; the tone of these was charmingly whimsical. He felt better. Warm. The frustration that came from her body pressed up against his was only temporarily problematic. It was sweet to him, really, that she knew so little about men.

The next day she seemed cheerful and energetic, delighting in the view from their window of the busy street—the pavement slicked with rain, and the storefronts, the Londoners with their spectrum of umbrellas. The air was blustery, the gray of the city tinged toward silver. For breakfast they had beans and toast at a café, both of them drinking too much of the strong coffee, musing about what to do and see first.

But in the street, Sheila noticed some of the British girls' outfits—they wore tall boots and short plaid kilts—and complained that she didn't have anything that was in style here to wear. Did he mind shopping for a while? she asked. Inside one of the shops, she tried on a pair of black boots like the ones she'd admired, with several different skirts. After each change she stood in front of the dressing room, modeling for him. The last thing she tried on was a pink cocktail dress that had caught her eye on the way in. It was skintight, more daringly cut than what she usually wore. She frowned at her image in the mirror hanging against the wall and in the reflection met his eye. Did he like it? Yes, very much, he told her. He reached out and took the edge of the silky hem between his fingertips.

"You would."

A whisper; hostile. He quickly withdrew his hand. Though he was sitting in a chair beside the dressing room door, he felt as if he were about to lose his balance, his vision of her back and reflection in the mirror momentarily blurred into one pale, many-limbed mass. But then in a casual tone she said she looked weird in pink, laughed; disappeared inside the dressing room. He wondered if he'd imagined the tone from before. They bought the clothes and shoes, and went back to the hotel to drop off the bags. She changed into the boots and a red-and-black kilt and took his hand as they stepped back out into the street. They spent the rest of the morning at the Tate.

When, in the afternoon, they returned to the hotel for a nap, he tried again. This time he was both more controlled and aggressive, coaxing her with more strategized kissing and massaging, trying to both ease and hurry her through it, thinking once they worked their way past the beginning she'd be fine. He had expected the first time would hurt her, but he hadn't yet gone inside her when her face changed. At first, he didn't see it as hate. He saw her screaming, her mouth gaping strangely open, before he heard the sound. Then she slapped his face. He did not move off her quickly enough, was too stunned, and just as he began to lean back she struck him again, this time catching his left temple, almost knocking him off balance. Before he could climb off of her she'd wriggled out from beneath him. He was shocked and ashamed. He'd never before tried to make a woman do something she didn't want to do sexually. But here was his wife, his *wife*, making him feel like a rapist. She scooted away from him—moving backward, her eyes all the while trained on his body—until she had her back against the headboard of the king-size bed. There, she looked down at him across an expanse of white sheets and hugged her knees. Tears ran down her face. "I'm sorry, but I can't," she said. "Sorry," she repeated. "I'm sorry." She looked, impossibly, as if she wanted to be held and also as if she might never want to be held again. He trembled as he made his way from the bed to the desk chair. There, naked, cold in the draft from the vent, he'd put his head in his hands and listened to her cry. He understood that while she didn't want him near her, he couldn't leave her alone in the room. He got up and switched on the TV and both of them stared at the flickering screen.

————

The man was the uncle who'd been sent away from the wedding, whom Jake had, because he was getting dressed, not actually seen. When, wanting some form to which to attach his rage, he asked what the man looked like, she said he was tall and thin, with dark hair. That these adjectives might also have described Jake bothered him a little; but then that was silly, lots of men fit that description. She added that the man had had a damaged eye, that he'd been in an accident, had had reconstruction work, which caused the place where iris met pupil to look jagged, "like a starburst," she said. The abuse had consisted mostly of heavy petting, no actual penetration, but because Sheila had been raised in such a conservative household, the psychological damage was profound, insinuated the therapist. It was about contrast, Jake gathered.

She'd been twelve. The uncle and his wife didn't have children and had invited her to stay with them in the summer at their home in North Carolina, while her parents went on a mission trip to Lugansk. Apparently he'd worked from the home. His wife worked in some office, and during her absence he'd let Sheila watch movies and listen to music her parents prohibited. He had also let her drink. The wife had come home early one day and found Sheila walking through the living room in her panties.

"We'd been listening to music in the bedroom," she said. "I'd never heard Bob Dylan before, and he thought he was amazing, and I was laughing at him because back then Bob Dylan's voice seemed so bad to me. He said we were going to listen until I understood."

She had been crying intermittently as she spoke, but now her lips turned into something near a smile. The therapist uncrossed her legs. Sheila's smile faded.

"And I'd gone out to the kitchen to get a drink. Aunt Mira looked like she was about to say hi to me, but then she didn't say anything. She just stared at my legs, like she was confused. Finally she said, 'What are you doing?' in a normal voice, and I said, 'Listening to music.' And she said, 'Where is your uncle?' And I knew we were going to get in trouble, but I couldn't think of what to say. I took too long and I guess she saw it in my face, and you could hear it coming from the bedroom— the stereo, I mean. She went after him then. Then she came back out to me, where I was still standing in the living room, not knowing what to do. I felt frozen. She looked like she wanted to say something to me, but instead she threw up. She was standing on a nice rug, and I remember how she leaned over to throw up on the hardwood floor instead of the rug.

"My parents came the next day, and my dad went back there into the room after my aunt told them what had happened— I thought he was going to kill him—but when he came back into the kitchen where we were, just a few minutes later, he said my uncle was in a ball on the floor and wouldn't get up. I remember him saying that. My mother wanted to know if I'd asked my uncle a lot of questions. She said to my aunt that she had noticed I had a habit of being *interested.* In other people. And I thought, *What does that even mean? Who's not interested in other people?* Even my aunt looked at her funny. She was so tired. By then she just wanted my mom to shut up."

In the car, riding home, her mother asked if she'd let her uncle touch her, and she said no. "That was exactly how she said it. *Let,*" Sheila said. "He only used his hands, he always had his clothes on, but I told her not at all. My dad didn't talk the whole time. At home he walked around with this blank look on his face. For days. And for a while he wouldn't really look at me when we talked. We never saw them again. My dad talked to my aunt on the phone every once in a while, at Christmas."

After that her mother never treated her the same. "She tried to make sure my dad and I were never alone together in the house. She thought I didn't notice, but I did. I noticed all the time. Once, I came back from a sleepover and a pair of my underwear must have fallen out of my bag in the hall, and an hour later she was in my bedroom, waving it in my face. She was almost screaming at me. It was like she thought I left it out *on purpose*."

She again broke into tears. He was baffled. He hadn't picked up on any animosity between her and her mother.

"He was so unhappy. He acted bored around my aunt, around everyone else, but when we were alone together he got happy. He said Aunt Mira hated him because they couldn't have children, even though the reason they couldn't have them had to do with her. Because of how she'd gotten hurt in the car accident they were in. He said just *seeing* me made him happy. He said I was so pretty.

"My mom hated the word. Pretty. When I was little, if I asked her if I was pretty, she'd say, 'It doesn't matter whether or not you're pretty. Beauty comes from being pure of heart.' She was right. She was trying to be a good mother. I understood that. I don't understand why I liked to hear it from him so much. I guess until then I thought I wasn't. But he said I was. He said it was too early for most people to see but that they would."

Her arms had been folded across her chest. Now she drew her legs onto the chair, clasped her hands around them. "That night, at my aunt and uncle's, after my aunt saw me, I woke up and he was sitting on the floor, staring at me. I didn't know if it was for real or a dream. I was sleeping on the couch in the living room and Aunt Mira was over in the kitchen. The dining room was between them and I couldn't see her, but I could see the light from the kitchen shining into it. She'd been in there most of the night. It was weird but it smelled to me like she was cooking stuff. I didn't go in there. So she was awake. I felt so bad for her. And when I opened my eyes and saw him sitting there watching me I just shut them again and pretended to be asleep because I didn't know what else to do. He sniffed. Then he was quiet. But I could feel him watching me. He was there for so long. I wanted him to go away. But also I didn't. Nobody looked at me the way he did. I hate being looked at."

"By everyone?" the therapist said. "Or just by men?"

Now Sheila turned to Jake. She wiped her mouth with the back of her hand. Her lips were paler. She turned to the therapist. He thought that the therapist was excited. It had something to do with the way she leaned forward ever so slightly and seemed to be trying to keep, rather than actually feeling, the patient, attentive expression. She said that Sheila was doing a wonderful "job," that both of them were doing "wonderful jobs," but that for now they needed to alter the dynamic in order to get the best results.

After that Sheila attended the sessions alone.

Time passed. He considered annulment but not seriously. He still loved her and thought that with time, through standing by her, he could show her that his love had to do with much more than sex. He couldn't stay married to a woman who wouldn't have sex with him *forever*. But he could wait.

He tried to throw himself into his new job—which consisted of writing speeches and press releases—and spent a lot of time in his office, a generous space in a wing of the hospital that

had once been used for patients. Because of this, the office included a bathroom, which meant he could in the afternoons,
after meetings, work for extensive periods of time without
having to go into the hall. He'd long ago learned to control
his emotions in order to work, and here, in his solitude, she'd
be reduced to a mood, to a gray film through which he saw the
important matters at hand. But occasionally the mood would
grow too thick to see through; then he'd get light-headed,
sweaty. If it was already dark he'd go out and find a place to
smoke about the grounds. If it was day, since the hospital had
a new no-smoking policy that he himself had formally pro-
moted, he'd have to retreat into the white-tiled emptiness of the
little bathroom to sit on the floor, back pressed against the
wall, and wait for calm.

He would always be waiting for something, it seemed. In
certain moods the thought of it was beautiful, but more frequently he wondered if his ideals were ridiculous. There, in
the little bathroom, trying not to think of Sheila, who often
couldn't quite mask her disappointment when he came home,
he began to fantasize about female coworkers: a gamine in-
tern; an older woman in marketing who'd brushed up against
him; Rachel Delaney, whom he'd met at a hospital-wide meeting, who with her husband donated huge amounts of money to
the system, who had almost died of cancer but now appeared
so well to him. Rachel Delaney especially.

She hadn't looked to him at all like the other wealthy donors,
with their tailored suits and designer shoes. Her ash-colored
hair was pulled up messily, in a big plastic clip, and she wore
a cheap black T-shirt with her skirt. The skirt was actually
elegant, silk and embroidered, but the flip-flops worn ragged.

At first, when his supervisor introduced them, during a break in the meeting, he hadn't noticed she was pretty. He listened and nodded as she spoke, struggling to focus after what had been his fifth meeting that day. Then she suddenly fell silent and rummaged around in her purse. She brought out a square of dark chocolate and popped it in her mouth. "Sorry," she said. "Chocolate's the only thing I can take to keep me from smoking. Did you ever smoke?"

He quit before he got married, he explained.

"I know it's not the healthiest way, but nothing else works. The only problem is that now I'm overweight. But when you've gone through what I've been through you pretty much have to surrender your vanity."

"You don't look overweight to me."

"Too little muscle mass and too much fat. You wouldn't be able to tell unless you saw me naked."

Her figure was lovely, and he blushed at the thought of her nudity. When she noticed she looked momentarily pleased, almost smiled.

"I identify with fat people," she went on. "I identify with the dying, because I had cancer once and will probably get it again. I was also addicted to painkillers, and so I identify with addicts. I've been poor, and believe me when I say I can fathom murder; murder unfortunately is no mystery to me," she rambled on, her eyes darting all over him before briefly meeting his own, only to again make their nervous cycles. "My ability to sympathize is so overwhelming that I find it more and more difficult to walk down the street, to have simple human interactions. But because I've got this ability—this ability to sympathize—I feel guilty for shutting it down. Which in itself becomes another, near-unbearable type of tension. Even now

I'm trying to resist what I see when I look in your eyes. Some-times I fantasize about bashing out my brains against a brick wall."

At this Jake started. Looked to see if anyone else was listen-ing. Nobody was. Then a VP interrupted them, and she moved away to talk to someone else. He was glad. She seemed to him mildly insane. But then, the next day, at a coffee shop, he'd had an unusual craving for dark chocolate—he didn't even really like chocolate—and bought a bar, thinking of her and, yes, picturing her naked. Now he couldn't help but think of her when he smoked.

At home, his wife began to lock herself in the bedroom to do special exercises recommended by the therapist. She was, as he understood it, learning to masturbate without shame. She seemed cheerful, even playful, when she came back down-stairs. With the exception of hugging and light kissing, they'd hardly touched since their honeymoon, and moved about the house so politely that he felt relieved by unexpected noise: the hum of the air conditioner switching on, her flushing the toilet upstairs, the neighbors slamming the door to their car. And though they slept in the same bed their bodies remained apart. But now she began to come up behind him and run her fingers through his hair, the way she used to, before, and she no longer stiffened when he held her. He felt relieved. When he intercepted a call about two missed therapy appoint-ments, he felt confused, but not worried. Her explanations for missing them—stuck in roadwork, an orchestra practice running over—were plausible.

One January afternoon, during the first flurry of a light snow, she called him at work, saying she needed him to come home, and surprised him at the door in the same black lingerie she had worn during their honeymoon. In bed, when he tentatively put his mouth between her legs—hopeful, but still a little afraid he might at any moment be slapped—she let him. Things were normal. Or, they were wonderful: the warm house and bed and the snow falling outside the upstairs window.

The next day the roads were too bad for him to drive to work, and they enjoyed what he thought of as their delayed honeymoon. That evening, as he lay back on the bed, happily exhausted and amused that they'd actually somehow torn away not only the sheets but the mattress cover, she sighed with what he at first mistook for contentment, and said, "I guess that's it, then."

"What? What's it?" He sat up, confused. She'd seemed to enjoy herself even more than he'd expected she would, it being her first time; he was almost sure she had come.

She was not on the bed but standing beside it, leaning against the wall with her arms crossed. She'd put on one of his white undershirts. She'd gotten leaner after the wedding; at dinner she seemed to eat less than half of what she herself put on the plate.

"You know. Sex. I mean, it's fun. But I thought . . ." She looked away from him, over at the basket in the corner where they put their dirty clothes. She hadn't done laundry in a while, apparently, and clothes spilled over the basket. "I thought it would feel more . . . it just feels so . . . *physical.*"

Of course it felt physical. It was sex, he said, laughing nervously. What did she mean?

"I expected a spiritual element," she explained. "I expected it to be physical and spiritual."

He felt as if she'd struck him again; his whole body rather than just his head. "You mean you don't feel anything for me." He stared down at the mattress, the pale gray stripes exposed.

"No. No. I love you . . . I just . . . it's me. I try to look in your eyes and I can't, and I know I'm supposed to, but I can't. It's fun, though. It's great. It's just me, is all. I shouldn't have said anything. I talk too much."

"Sheila." He looked up at her. She stared straight ahead now, lost in thought. "Did you stop seeing your therapist?"

She pulled her arms more tightly against her chest and looked into his eyes, shifted her gaze again to the laundry pile. "No."

She was lying, it seemed to him.

"Okay," he said gently.

She climbed back onto the bed and curled up against him, her head on his chest, her red hair spilling over his arm. "I didn't mean to ruin everything," she said quietly. "I'm sorry."

III

He lost track of her early in the night, when, as some coworkers approached from one direction, Sheila darted off in the other with the excuse of needing another ginger ale. He chatted with them—some women from the marketing department, two of whom were young and pretty and seemed girlishly aware of their party appearances, hands fidgeting with bracelets and smoothing hair, bodies moving in the formal dresses with a self-consciousness he'd never have glimpsed at work. Though he had trouble following the conversation, he managed to hide it. How much time had passed? Fifteen minutes? Thirty?

The women moved on.

In the far corner of the next room (crowded, red walls) he spotted his host and hostess talking to another couple. Rachel's husband, a bearded man with a lot of coarse blond hair, seemed to be telling a story, mock-scowling and making exaggerated gestures. But while the couple grinned back, Rachel stared blankly past him, hand cupping a full glass of red wine. The room had two openings and at that moment, from the other side, a child in a white flannel nightgown—Rachel's daughter, the one who'd come to his office—streaked from one opening to the other, a weirdly determined look on her face. Rachel began to hurry after her, yelling her name, the anger in her voice belied by the sudden pleasure in her expression. As she passed near him she met his eye and raised her brows so that he felt included in the child's mischief, the mother's pursuit. For a moment he forgot where he was going. But as she vanished from his sight he again became aware of the problem, his search.

There were many familiar faces—doctors and administrators, board members and their spouses—but also plenty of people he didn't recognize. Laughter would erupt from one cluster, and then the next. Many of them, though youthful and well preserved in the way of successful people in a mid-size town, were much older than he. There was talk of time-shares in Europe, of health-care legislation, of encounters with unruly patients. He smiled and nodded his way through.

Where was she? He made his way through a number of rooms, still sipping at the now-watery gin and tonic he'd gotten when he first arrived. At the bar, he got another. He passed through the kitchen, where the waitstaff was replacing trays with hors d'oeuvres, and moved out onto the broad back deck overlooking a little courtyard, a fountain. Out here white lights were strung up around the tree branches that grew along the walls, and people's faces were harder to make out. The early spring air was neither hot nor cold. He studied the throng of bodies, but he could not find his wife's face. He leaned against the railing and looked down into the court-yard. Below he glimpsed the little girl, now standing by the fountain that shimmered beneath the strung lights. Her pale hair, in the surrounding dimness, gleamed white by the glow of the water. She turned her face up toward the balcony, met his eye. Then, from the lower part of the house, from some-where beneath the deck, a female voice that was not her mother's called out to her, and she darted into the shadows. He waited for a moment to see if she'd return, but she was gone.

Now he found himself drawn into a nearby conversation.

"But I heard it was inherited," a man said.

Jake didn't recognize these people from work.

"No. I went to high school with them in Raleigh. Daniel's parents were teachers and Rachel's family was on welfare after her dad died. It was vacuum parts." There was a pause, the clink of ice. "They owned factories in South America. Made a killing. But then it came out that handling the parts caused birth defects. Nowadays all vacuum parts are like that, if you notice. There's usually a warning in the little instruction man-ual? You're supposed to be sure to wear gloves or wash your hands after. But this was a while back and a company that used their parts ended up getting sued by a customer. The company tried to file a suit against the Delaneys' company but it was proven that they knew what they were buying and Rachel and Daniel got out okay."

"I heard she had a nervous breakdown," a woman said in a low voice.

"From the guilt. I heard she thinks her cancer was punishment from God, and that's why they donate all that money."

"That's ridiculous," said a man wearing thick-rimmed glasses. "That's just a rumor."

"It amazed me that she let them write about her like they did—her treatments and reconstruction. I'd feel weird when people looked at me and just knew, well . . ."

"You couldn't beat the promotion they got for the center from that, though. That was smart. Nothing beats the personal-narrative stuff. People eat that shit up."

"Didn't she hire the designer, too? I like the paintings in the lobby there. Who is it who did those paintings?"

"The Japanese woman from Charleston?"

"No, it was someone local. Smythe or Simms or . . ."

The conversation veered into a discussion of the prices of local art. He turned and went back inside the house.

It had been afternoon when Rachel knocked on the door to his office. At first he hadn't answered, hoping whoever it was would go away. The little girl with her was very blond and wore a black pair of galoshes, with a gold-and-white jumper. She looked five or six, her eyes the water-blue of her mother's. Though it was March, Rachel wore another black T-shirt, and the same flip-flops, pale legs bare. Her long hair was pulled into the same plastic tortoiseshell clip.

"She knew you were in here," the little girl said.

"Violet," Rachel said in a warning voice. To him, "I don't mean to bother you, but I just wanted to talk about the press releases for the mammography unit, and . . ." She was looking around his office as she spoke, and now paused. "Does it bother you to work in here?"

"Why would it bother me?"

"It's just, this was a room for patients."

"So?"

"So people have suffered and died in here."

"People have died in here," the little girl repeated in a low, wondering voice.

"It's a hospital," he said in his most rational tone. He wanted them to leave, but Rachel was moving deeper in. She walked toward his window and began to speak of how this view of his must have been for a significant number of people a "last view of the world." The little girl began to pick up and examine objects on his desk: his brass paperweight, his Post-it notes, his pens. She looked at these things as if they were fantastic, turning them in her small white hands while the water-colored eyes contemplated their sides from multiple angles.

Now Rachel reached into her purse and extracted the chocolate, her back to him. He imagined her white skin beneath the thin black fabric of her shirt. He tried to think of something else but the only something else his mind would turn to was the deceased peering out of his window. His head ached. He did not feel well. He wanted a cigarette. The little girl, with a look of intense concentration, was sticking blank Post-it notes—pink, yellow, mint-green—all over his paperwork and desk. Her mother still stared out his window, out at the overcast afternoon. His office smelled of chocolate.

"Could I have some of that?" he said.

She turned from the window to smile at him. She stepped close to him, his head level with her waist, his eyes drawn to her breasts. With one hand she self-consciously wrapped her cardigan around her chest, and with the other handed him a square of the candy. She watched his face too long.

"I see," she said softly.

"See what?"

She reached out, as if to touch his cheek, but retracted her hand. He felt, still, as if she were touching him. She might have been touching him all over with the water-colored eyes: they wanted each other. Then she averted her gaze, broke the spell. "Violet, Mr. Harrison is tired and we need to get out of his hair now. Come back another time."

"Wait."

He quickly began to sift through the contents of his desk drawers for something that might interest the child. Found himself handing over pens, an old Rolodex, a small green clipboard bearing the logo of a pharmaceutical company. The child accepted these things with the air of one accepting precious gifts. Suddenly he had the feeling that all things in his office were sacred, were less and also more than what they were.

"That's all she can carry," the mother said, smiling. "Say thanks."

"Thank you," the child said to him, arms full of his things.

Gone.

He was very tired. He laid his head down on his desk, face buried in arms.

The upstairs of the house appeared smaller than he expected. Smaller and plainer. But that was probably because the hall was narrow and all of the doors shut. Would he really have to go around opening all these doors? And what would happen if someone saw him up here? They'd think he was being nosy.

What he imagined was opening the door to a bedroom, a guest room, perhaps, to find a couple embracing on a made-up bed. He imagined lamplight, auburn hair, her back turned to him. Some man fumbling with the zipper at the back of her dress.

He felt light-headed. He'd forgotten to eat anything. They could go to a diner, he thought, as soon as the party ended, after he found her. What he expected, as much as he expected to catch her with a man, was to go through all these rooms and find them empty, then go back down and run into her, find she'd been searching for him at the same time he'd been searching for her, and they'd simply kept missing each other, as they did sometimes after having drifted apart in the mall, at bookstores.

The first two doors opened to darkness, the hall light skimming the outlines of an office in one room, a treadmill and weight-lifting equipment in the other. Without thinking he opened a smaller door he should've known led to a linen closet.

The next door he opened brought him face-to-face with his hostess.

He started.

She showed no surprise, only amusement at, he guessed, his embarrassment, his getting caught. The child was with her.

"Strawberry," the child said to him.

They sat on a plain white cot. The room had polished hardwood floors and ivory walls bearing soft ellipses of light from two standing lamps on either side of the room. The only shadows that broke the light came from their bodies, for there was no furniture. Rachel's sweater lay in a black lump beside her, on the cot, her bare arms and shoulders exposed, the thin blue straps of the dress, perhaps because he was looking down at her, seeming to barely cover her nakedness. He quickly turned his eyes to the child in her white flannel gown, etched faintly with caramel-colored flowers, he saw now. Her blond hair looked mussed and after she said *strawberry* for the second time, she frowned.

"He doesn't know what we're playing," Rachel said to her. "He just thinks you're being weird. Tell him what we're playing."

"Word association," the little girl said to him. In a very serious voice, "I say a word, and you say the first word that comes to your mind, and then I say the first word that comes to my mind when I hear your word, and then you say—"

"He gets the point, Violet."

"Strawberry," the girl said again, insistently.

"Milk," he replied.

"Now Mommy."

"Cow."

"Hamburger," Violet said. To Jake, "Hamburger comes from cows. People kill the cows and then they eat them. They made me eat cows but I didn't know what it was," she said sadly. "I didn't know."

"Please don't start again, Violet," her mother said. "No one meant to taint you. No one knew how you'd feel about it." To Jake, "Her nanny doesn't know how to talk to sensitive children."

"I ate cows," the little girl persisted gravely.

"This is not the time for us to talk about that," Rachel said. "It's time for me to talk to Mr. Harrison now. Time for you to go."

"But I want to sleep in here with you tonight."

She latched on to her mother's bare arm and began to whimper. When Rachel gave her a threatening look, the child let go of her mother. She got up from the cot, stomped her small bare feet past Jake at the door, and in the dim hall burst into a sprint. He watched her open the door that faced theirs from the opposite end, flooding the space with light. Briefly he glimpsed a huge high-ceilinged room with a Ping-Pong table, beyond it a sofa and a big-screen television flashing the bright pastels of a cartoon. He heard the shrieks of children. Then the door slammed shut and the hall seemed twice as dark as before.

"Close the door behind you," Rachel told him.

When he turned back to face her, she was already pulling down the straps of the dress. Her blue eyes reflected what seemed to him one moment panic, the next anticipation. In the soft light and emptiness, the room might have been any room or every room he had ever known, and she had always been in this place that was also herself, waiting. The muted laughter from the party could no longer be heard. Faintly, the music he had not noticed below announced itself through the floor.

THREE FRIENDS IN
A HAMMOCK

In a hammock strung between the trunks of two trees, she told us the story of this friend of hers, X, whose boyfriend was a successful writer on whose cell phone she found texts and photos of himself he'd been sending to other women. He had sent the same texts and photos to two women. Copy-pasted them. Not even bothered to tailor them for each individual recipient. Both thought he was in love with them, and seemed to be in some state of waiting. In the other room he napped. When he woke and came out, X confronted him and told him he had mental problems. She told my friend she was the only one close enough to him to be able to tell him, and in the way my friend described it, I intuited X had taken pride in being the woman to tell him the problem of who he was.

I understood X must have wanted to think she was not like the other women who thought her boyfriend was in love with them. Wanted to think she had some upper hand on the reality of the situation. Maybe she did.

I knew what it was like to have found out some vital information about the person in the next room that he wouldn't want you to have, and I also knew what it was like to be the one to whom such information was presented. I thought of how we try to tell people, *I am the one who really loves you*, maybe most especially when we are not sure that person loves us.

I am the one who really loves you. I see you. I see how fucked-up you are at a level no one else can and therefore I see more of you and therefore I love you more.

But so then someone really loving you might be a good reason to avoid that person.

All three of us were divorced or about to be legally so. All three of us were artists. All three of us had left.

The architect ex-husband of the woman telling the story watched us from the deck. The evening I'd been introduced to him, back when he and the woman telling the story of X were married, I'd felt infatuated with him at first sight, thinking they were brother and sister. *But that man is a little in love with his sister*, I'd thought back then, seeing it as a drawback. Now I thought, *You can never go out with him because of your connection to these two.* Now at this party, back in the kitchen, before we'd gone outside to the hammock, I hadn't wanted to stand too close to him or have a conversation. One other man drew my attention, but not enough of it. I was decidedly with the two friends and more than once someone else regarded us as a sort of entity. All three of us were attractive but insecure and attracted to each other. The woman next to me had held my hand once when we walked out of a bar and had told me a story about the woman on the other side of her taking her hand in the same way as she then held mine. I had been happy and uncomfortable. A question I could not articulate was implied. I pretended it had not been asked. I have difficulty in being close to people, and as she held my hand I went outside myself, already analyzing what was happening before having experienced it. *She is holding my hand*, a voice in my head observed. It was night. We passed the fronts of closed shops. The city had strewn the trees along that street with strings of clear, minute lights, like the lights on Christmas trees. I said something about how even men who were friends held hands in parts of Europe, feeling only slightly detached from my own voice.

In the hammock the friend next to me, the one in the middle, sat with her leg pressed against mine. Earlier that day she had said my friend on the other side of her and I both were her best friends but I knew from day to day and even moment to moment alliances shifted. You can't be equally close to two people at the same time. Her body pressed against mine and not against the body of our friend on the other side of her but this was only because I was taller and both of us heavier than the other friend, who was short and slight, and because the shorter, slighter friend held herself poised in such a way to keep herself from sliding into the friend in the middle. (Though months later, in speaking of the incident, the one in the middle would during dinner bring up that I'd sat stiffly beside her that day in the hammock, avoiding pressing against her, while the other friend unselfconsciously slid into her; which I believe at some point did happen too.) Because the friend in the middle was so close to me, I more frequently gazed across her to meet the eyes of the friend at her other side, the one who'd told the story of X and her unfaithful boyfriend. When she told stories about other people, her eyes flashed. Ever since she had come into the presence of the ex-husband—who was frequently from the deck watching us—she had become younger and bolder and not like the more scattered, unsure version of herself she'd been that morning, when we'd been somewhere else. I was not best friends with her. She lived out of town. But I fantasized about moving to her city, and maybe I would. Then when the friend between us came to visit she would be the one from out of town. Her other best friend and I would have grown closer. We would all be "best" friends. In the mindset I was in (am frequently in) there were a number of foreseeable complications.

During the separation from my husband I woke up crazy with paranoia, and I was mad at everyone because I suspected they had found in me unforgivable fault. I doubted they would attend my funeral but reassured myself that dead I wouldn't care. When people I had in my head broken up with would send spirited replies to emails I'd sent two days before, back when I'd still thought of us as connected (before they had not attended my imaginary funeral) I felt stupid and relieved.

We lay in the hammock at the end of summer. The uncomfortable sense of feeling pressed into the body of my friend by the slope of the hammock was also very pleasurable. I hadn't chosen to sit that close. She and I had slid into that position as we submitted to the physics of the hammock situation. Two of us were pale with freckles. Two of us had dark hair and green eyes. One of us had blue eyes. One of us was tall and two of us were short and two of us were skinny. One of us had large breasts. One of us didn't talk to her mother and one of our fathers had left and one of our sets of parents had not divorced. One of us wrote. One of us painted abstracts. One of us played cello still and one had stopped. One of us put ads on Craigslist asking for male models for short films and photographs and paid the models (who were not professionals) ten dollars an hour. Our work sold. Two of us had at some point had agoraphobia and all of us had problems with depression and anxiety and one of us had tried to kill herself and one of us had been raped and one of us had been molested and two of us had small aged white dogs and one of us had a kid. At the kid's last birthday party the opened presents that would go to her father's house went into one pile and the ones that would go to her mother's in another. Each of us had slept with a man that one of the others had also slept with. One of us had woken in the middle of the night with one of those men, furiously watched his sleeping body, and contemplated leaving because in her dreams she'd become convinced that he'd have preferred to be sleeping with the other, but then she had gone back to sleep.

All three of us could disassociate for long periods of time and then, snapped back to our surface, be unaware of what had been happening, and for how long we'd been away.

When one of my two friends asked me a question or seemed to understand what I was saying I had trouble believing this was really happening. Intermittently each of them would seem impossibly beautiful, too beautiful to be real and nearby. I could not decide if my husband had really loved me. His face and body as he sat in a chair in this little room we sat in with my lawyer before going into court kept flashing in my mind. Back in the kitchen watching my friend with her ex-husband I could not decide whether or not I wished they would get back together. She missed him. She spoke of him, of leaving him, as if an irrevocable mistake had been made. In the kitchen they spoke Albanian with each other. They stood several feet apart. Not knowing the words, I saw only people making sounds at each other, filling the kitchen with atmospheric perfume. I could not decide whether or not people had ever *really* loved each other if they could stop loving each other. I could not decide if love was real as a thing or something that could never entirely be proven, like God, and could only be experienced in the act of reaching and so in retrospect would always fall in doubt. I could not decide if I could love and be loved factually. At some time in my life the words *I love you* had seemed like a revelation, not a reason to brace myself for its withdrawal.

One of us was telling another story, a story that had come to mind in response to the story of X. I pushed my foot against the ground to get the hammock swinging (gently). The cook-out was for someone's birthday—the brother of my friend's ex-husband—and the sound of the others singing "Happy Birthday" to him startled all three of us to look ahead, to recall the context of the party, to remember it was Armend's birthday, and that there were a bunch of other people at the opposite end of the yard.

THE WAY YOU
MUST PLAY ALWAYS

I

From the window Gretchen could see her dad's car round the curb. The disappearance of it gave her a sense of sudden looseness, as if the weight of her body no longer pressed her to the bench in quite the same way. Safe, she thought. Saved. Because Miss Grant did not plan to tell her parents what had happened last week. She'd neither called nor gone after Gretchen's dad in the drive, as Gretchen feared she might. She as usual sat in her frumpy old chair and told Gretchen to begin the week's piece. Anxiously she fingered the fried black tips of her hair and avoided Gretchen's eyes, or maybe Gretchen avoided hers. She cleared her throat and said, "*Tempo.* Notice the *tempo.*"

So they were going to act as if nothing had happened.

The love inside her had room to spread out now. It was part nervousness, part desperation, and a little craziness too, and she felt it begin to rush outside of her and around her, leaving invisible prints of itself all over the things she touched: her bag, her books, the keys, the pages of the music she turned. She wore a silk print dress, inappropriate for lessons both because of its fanciness and the fact that it was dirty, and crossed and uncrossed then crossed her legs again, just to feel the silk.

"You didn't practice," Miss Grant said, oblivious to Gretchen's excitement. Maybe oblivious to all excitement except the cool intensity of her music.

Now that she knew Miss Grant would not tell on her, she felt especially bold. "I don't care anymore," she said. She would've hated Miss Grant for telling, but also hated her now, because she hadn't.

Miss Grant bristled. "Don't care about *what* exactly?"

"Anything." Gretchen laughed then, to make the word a joke rather than a challenge, because what if Miss Grant did get mad and tell after all?

Miss Grant sighed. "Let's try the right hand alone."

Gretchen focused on the notes this time, noted the three-quarter time, the sharp. But every other measure she played the wrong notes on purpose and eyed Miss Grant askance.

"You're only hurting yourself," Miss Grant told her.

Gretchen didn't enjoy piano, not really. Her mother had put her up to lessons she wished she'd had herself. "My span isn't wide enough," her mom said, waving her fingers, which were cracked and dry from the frequent washings her nursing job required. "You could be a concert pianist though. You have the *fingers*." But the true catalyst for the lessons was that she'd a little over a year ago gotten into trouble, and her parents had thought the piano would "ground" her.

The trouble was that Gretchen's grandma had found her alone with her cousin Jamie in the basement of her grandma's house during a family get-together. They had some of their clothes off. Her grandma, sick with the beginnings of dementia, but, on that particular day, lucid, took it in stride. "Kissing cousins," she said after she delivered the news in full to their parents. Her voice shook but she smiled. "Happens all the time."

"It sounds like more than kissing, Mama," her dad said. He turned red in the face and clenched his hands against the top of a chair, just as Gretchen's mom burst into tears.

It—the petting and probing and laughing in closed dim places—had happened several times before, in other rooms and houses (though Gretchen and Jamie weren't about to tell this to their family). Though Gretchen knew she shouldn't have snuck off with him, she still felt shocked by how seriously everyone took their relationship. Technically (barely), she was still a virgin. And she didn't love him, not exactly, didn't fantasize about the two of them marrying or spending their lives together, and didn't even like certain things about him, like the patchy beard he tried to grow, or the way he bit her ear too hard in passionate moments, or his hands inching beneath the elastic of her first real bra when she did not want to do *that again*, just talk. Did this make the situation more or less corrupt? she wondered. Because she'd gotten absolved too quickly to find out. No one seemed to want to think that Gretchen, who looked young even for her thirteen years, whose wide eyes invited motherly comments from strangers—*watch your step there, sweetie; this is very hot, dear; where is your coat?*—could be anything but a victim. Jamie, three years older and strange, was the deviant. Because he was already known for photographing decomposed outhouses in fields on the outskirts of town, watching *The Godfather* films over and over, and refusing to do school assignments he considered beneath him, their parents decided he'd pressured Gretchen into doing what they did. Really she couldn't remember if he'd touched her first. What she remembered was that during Thanksgiving and Christmas and Easter, while her mom had been busy giving advice to her divorced aunts on the porch, and her dad had gone off with her uncle to drink in the shed, whenever she'd said, "Look," or "Listen," Jamie had been the only one to see past the blur of casserole-covered tables and screaming toddlers and older girl cousins leaning into the boyfriends they'd brought, to notice her.

Because their families had begun to take turns attending holiday gatherings, and because his parents had immediately sent him away to an all-boys boarding school (to his father, his being with Gretchen had been the "last straw"), she had not seen him since they got caught. She imagined him brooding and sloppy in an expensive uniform, wandering around on a lawn beneath great old trees. Did he imagine her attending her new private Christian school, where most of the other students had known each other since kindergarten, and her relief that summer vacation had finally freed her of it? Did he imagine her playing piano?

She'd been taking lessons for a year now, and often wondered just how closely her parents had looked at her piano teacher when they'd decided *she* would be the one to "ground" Gretchen. Perhaps the word *Juilliard*, which they so liked saying to their friends, had somehow canceled out the piano teacher's weirdness.

But because her mom and dad desperately wanted the lessons to be successful, Gretchen didn't complain. Her parents already slept in separate rooms—it had started the year before—and though they'd explained it to her, that her dad talked in his sleep, she felt in her body the tremors of a bridge linking places much larger than itself together.

"Are you loving the piano?" her mom would say, adjusting her glasses, running a hand through her cropped gray hair.

"Yeah," Gretchen said, for they had little else safe to talk about these days, since Gretchen's mom, who'd never even dated anyone before her dad, wanted her to "open up" about all the things Gretchen least wanted to discuss.

Her dad, too, took a strong interest in the piano, his fingers sometimes reverentially skimming its wood, but never touching the keys. She could not bear to think of him knowing about what she had done with Jamie, and yet, whenever he stood near, the knowledge pressed continually at the sides of her thoughts.

"My favorite is Moonlight Sonata," he said one evening, leaning against the door, voice strangely tender, eyes present in a way to which she wasn't accustomed. "Can you play Moonlight Sonata?" he persisted.

"Not yet," she said, fingers lazing over the notes of a new scale that already bored her, looking away. "But I'll try to learn it, all right?"

Miss Grant had a pale pinched face, which grew even more pinched when she was angry. The muscles around her eyes often twitched and sometimes the muscle just above the left eyelid started up, making her look as if she were winking. The incongruity of the silly winking and the angry face made Gretchen want to laugh, but also to turn away. A dark dyed fringe cut across her forehead and fanned over her cheeks and flared out haphazardly in back. She rouged her cheeks with terracotta, which did not match the cool pearl of her skin. And she lined her eyes with oily kohl, the line too thick and sloppy to flatter.

Her silver bangles tinkled against one another when she moved her hand across Gretchen's composition book to write notes. The oversweet vanilla of her drugstore perfume hung about her like a cloud, so that even with a foot between them Gretchen felt pressed to Miss Grant's bosom, enveloped in her air. Sometimes, when she played all right, Miss Grant would pace behind the stool, in front of the window. She always had on tight black jeans and some kind of ruffled black silk blouse. Her high-heeled velveteen lace-ups clicked across the hard-wood floor.

They played in a butter-colored room with a giant picture window that overlooked the long-neglected bramble of Miss Grant's backyard. Plastic eggs, left from Easter, still hung from some of the trees and in the wind waved defiantly violet, pink, blue, and green above the weeds. With the exception of Miss Grant's chair, a worn wicker thing that looked as if it had been brought in from years of sitting in the yard, and a peach-colored sofa against the opposite wall, the room was empty.

Miss Grant had a white grand piano, "like John Lennon's," she'd remarked when Gretchen and her mother had first visited her house last summer. And on the top of the piano Miss Grant kept a small, framed photo of Mr. Lennon. In the photo, Lennon wore dark Amish-style clothing and stood in a field, alone. The photo looked carefully torn around the edges, and Gretchen wondered if it had been cut from a magazine. During her first lesson, in hopes of embarrassing Miss Grant, she had posed this question.

Miss Grant replied, rather unconvincingly, that it had not. Her words were crisp and carefully enunciated. The accent sounded artificially northern, and Gretchen imagined her practicing it alone in front of a mirror.

"Do you have a thing for him?" Gretchen moved her hand toward the frame, but Miss Grant pushed it from her reach.

"He's dead."

"So you like a dead guy?"

"Not in the way you're suggesting. I admire his"—she paused—"genius."

"I didn't know he was such a great piano player."

"Lots of people don't understand the charm of his rusticity. His playing was pure." She then asked if Gretchen would like to hear a song by him, for inspiration. She played "Imagine," a song Gretchen had heard on the oldies station, and that her mother had deemed sacrilegious because of the line, "Imagine there's no heaven." Miss Grant's long wiry fingers glided over the keys with a sound slightly different from the one on the radio; the notes matched, but the style was more assertive, the harmony thicker, with flourishes here and there that made up for the absence of the words. Her nails were lacquered a dark red, like her lips. With the red lips and her paleness and black fringe, she resembled a distorted Snow White. In the middle of the song she closed her eyes, parted her lips, and swayed a little, which made Gretchen suddenly anxious to leave the room. After she finished playing she was glassy-eyed and quiet. She whispered that she needed to step outside to get the mail.

"The mail?"

"It was late today."

Really she was out there smoking, in the drive, her clothes absurdly black against the heat that rose from the pavement. Gretchen could see only by standing at the edge of the window, looking out at the most extreme angle. Inside, Miss Grant did not even think to make up an excuse for not holding any letters, but Gretchen let it pass, just because she could.

———

Miss Grant had moods. Sometimes, for most of the lesson she stared out the window while Gretchen played. If Gretchen said something unsolicited, a startled look would pass over her face and she'd fold or unfold her skinny black-clad legs and say, "Pardon?" But when Gretchen actually played something well, Miss Grant frightened her. For example, a few months ago, when she'd been craving Jamie still, and let her yearning for him slip into Nocturne in E, Miss Grant had jumped up from her chair and shaken Gretchen's shoulders, gazed intensely into her eyes, and said, "Do you feel it? There was purity in that, Gretchen. This is the way you must play always." She held Gretchen's shoulders too long, long fingernails digging into her skin, and Gretchen had had to pull away, feeling ashamed. She had excused herself to the bathroom and Miss Grant had stepped outside.

Fiona Xiu was Miss Grant's only other student. She had started lessons last June, a month after Gretchen. Fiona looked Chinese but sounded American. Sometimes, when she arrived early for her lesson and had to wait on the peach sofa, her hair caught the light from the window and hung against her shoulders like a sleek, glossy curtain. In the summer her broad cheekbones also took on a sheen, but in the winter they turned dry, almost powdery. On every reasonably bright day she waved at the dust particles in the shaft of sunlight that cut in diagonally from the window. The waving distracted Gretchen. She could not help but be more interested in Fiona than the song she played and could not help but turn to watch her every minute or so. She watched Fiona crazily batting the air, and she envied her shoes, which looked strappy and sexy and womanlike.

They had begun lessons around the same time, but Fiona played from a level 4 book, while Gretchen played from a level 2.

Every now and then, when Miss Grant had to get a drink or go to the bathroom or step outside, she left them alone together. Fiona's sentences were peppered with the word "fuck." She'd played "Für Elise" "a hundred fucking times." The weather was fucking hot. Her new espadrilles were fucking cheap. When Gretchen had once slipped and said, "Fuck," her parents went hysterical. But, according to Fiona, when she said it in front of Mrs. Xiu, she just frowned. Mr. Xiu didn't even care. Fiona said this was because they were "fobby."

Perhaps Miss Grant had shaken Fiona's shoulders too, and said, *This is the way you must play always*. If Miss Grant had done this, Gretchen would feel relieved, but also disappointed. More relieved than disappointed though, because playing well didn't suit her. To play well—what Miss Grant seemed to think of as well—you had to put an ache into the music, a kind of happy-misery that made the music but also came from it. And so playing well in front of people humiliated Gretchen, like getting caught with Jamie (her grandmother watching, the shaft of light from the door, Jamie not even *knowing* to look up until she told him). And if she wasn't going to play in front of people, what was the point of playing at all? She didn't see it. Playing well was for someone like Miss Grant. Someone who had a crush on a dead guy she didn't even know.

"You will not wear that dress," her mother had said at home. "You've worn it to church twice in a row." Though Gretchen had gone on sorting through the hamper of dirty clothes for the dry cleaner's. She had sprayed the dress with air freshener while her mom yelled on, her voice trying to sound hard instead of scared.

Now she crossed and uncrossed her legs, felt the smooth swish of the silk, however unfresh, against her knees.

As she played (lazily, poorly) she could hear only the clink of the keys and could not listen for the sounds that might have drifted from down the hall, from the room where Miss Grant's brother stayed. To her the song was like a little prison of sound.

II

The bathroom itself was unremarkable, distasteful with out-dated hair products and mildewed tiles. But the hallway in-trigued her. It smelled not bad, but stale and closed and faintly sweet, like the house of a very old person, not a young person like Miss Grant. The brown-and-gold paisley wallpaper was peeling and yellowed with moisture around the edges, and the look of it matched the smell of the hall. Unlike her hallway at home, there were no pictures of children or beaches or family reunions. All of the doors along the hall were shut (Gretchen's parents had an open-door rule), and this made her crazy with curiosity. She had expected Miss Grant's doors to shield se-crets. Maybe a shrine to John Lennon, of the sort the psychos liked in the crime-investigation shows her parents watched. Maybe a journal describing Miss Grant's sins. Maybe a cold, dark emptiness, like the look that flitted over Miss Grant's features from time to time.

It had been no less than a month ago when she heard him.

Miss Grant had gone outside, Gretchen to the bathroom, like any other day. And she had heard a muffled cough. At first she thought Miss Grant had gotten a little dog. She cracked the door—the last door—and found a man.

He was a slender, almost gaunt man in a white-and-green-checked bathrobe, lying on his side on the bed, the sheets half twisted off the mattress. The overhead light was not on, but sunlight streamed through the half-open blinds and fell in diagonals across the bed. The man held a homemade cigarette to his lips, the smoke of which smelled like dirt. He took her in with calm curiosity, gave her an all-over glance, and said, "Hey."

His presence so surprised her that she didn't say anything for a minute, just stared at him, and the cigarette he held, the thin snake of smoke that straightened and disappeared just past his head. He held it not the usual way, but between his thumb and index finger. "Is that pot?" she said finally.

The man bolted upright against the headboard and raised his eyebrows. "Absolutely not."

He wore nothing beneath his robe, and she could see the dark blond fuzz of his chest. Despite the fact that part of his wavy, wheat-colored hair had been shaved off, and that the lack of hair revealed an odd, dimpled, stitched-over stretch of scalp, he had a strikingly handsome face. His eyes were the color of the mint juleps her father, despite her mother's protest, drank on summer weekends—the color of mint leaves submerged in bourbon. His prominent nose had obviously been broken once, which made him seem especially masculine.

"It is, isn't it?"

"So what? I have a brain tumor. I can do whatever I want."

Philosophically, this intrigued her. He was watching porno on TV. (She didn't know a lot about porno, but knew enough to recognize it.) A couple doing it in an office, in a chair. With his remote, the man stopped the show, so that the screen went blue. He grinned and bent toward her. His grin looked knowing, sly, revealed a set of straight, lightly stained teeth. He reached out and gently poked her shoulder. Something in her belly stirred, this due not to his touch but to his smell. He did not smell good. But something in his musk, part dirt like the joint he smoked, part winey and sweet, made her want to put her face to his neck, the way she had with Jamie.

At that moment Miss Grant appeared in the doorway, a pale floating face in the blackness of her clothes and the shadow of the hall. "Please go back to the piano room. Now." Then, lower, almost whispering to him, *I'm trying here, Wes. I'm really trying.*

"But she let herself in. I didn't think she was real."

"Why wouldn't she be real?" Miss Grant said, voice cracking. She threw her hands up in the air. The man shrugged and half collapsed against the headboard. Miss Grant whirled around, scowling, and ushered Gretchen out into the hall. Out of the room, she made a weak smile and said that she was very sorry if her brother had said anything strange to her. "He isn't feeling well."

In the piano room Gretchen played "Blue Swing." Miss Grant introduced G-sharp minor. Gretchen played this a few times, and then it was time to go. As she rose from the stool Miss Grant placed her hand on Gretchen's shoulder, her touch awkward and clammy and a bit too forceful. She must have thought that Gretchen would tell her parents about what had happened. To Gretchen, the idea of this—of her telling her mom about the man—was almost laughable.

She thought of him all the long summer week, she alone in the house with *them* at work, lying in bed past noon to imagine what she might have said to sound older. Mostly elderly people and yuppies lived in their neighborhood, and two of the three streets led to dead ends, but still she'd sometimes put on her clothes and walk slowly about with the ridiculous (she knew) idea that he might for some reason drive through. When she found the remnants of someone's late-night party—cigarettes, beer bottles—in the more private cul-de-sac, by the woods, she thought how easily he might slip down to meet her while all the people who would stop such a meeting slept. Except he was sick. Would he get well? When? She had no one to confide in. Her few friends from school were on exotic vacations of the sort her parents would never take her on (in August they spent a week at Pawleys Island, as they had for the past fourteen years of her life). And so the sleeping late and sweaty walks and quiet desire melted into a thick, heady dream.

Usually, in the evening, her parents jarred her awake with eager, needy voices. Tortured her with their idea of "family togetherness" time, which was watching crime-investigation shows while eating pizza. The shows featured grave detectives hunting down crack dealers and serial killers and questioning prostitutes. Her father, who worked at City Hall, enjoyed catching flaws in the shows' details. "That's not how it happens," he'd yell authoritatively at the actor on the screen, causing her to start. And so she couldn't even understand the point of them watching it. Usually she slipped away fifteen minutes into a show, after she'd finished her pizza. (Though too often one of them would notice her absence and at the foot of the stairs beckon to her in a jokey or irritated voice, until she returned, only to leave again, the cycle inescapable.) But that week, she forced herself to sit with them through two shows so that during commercials she could ask her mom speculative questions about brain tumors. Apparently the issue was far more complicated than she realized, and her questions led only to more questions. To divert suspicion she finally had to say she found a bump on her head. Her mom looked amused rather than worried, but said, "Let's check." With the same fingers she used to go through Gretchen's drawers and closet while Gretchen was out—like one of the detectives from the show, looking for clues that would reveal Gretchen's sinister element—she probed Gretchen's scalp. Her gentle-intelligent-suspicious fingers made Gretchen want to cry.

"That's not how it happens," her dad snapped happily at the TV, making things normal again.

But next lesson she didn't see him. Miss Grant did not go out to smoke. She lingered in the hall when Gretchen went to use the bathroom. When he finally showed himself, it felt like a miracle, although he was just passing through the piano room to get to the kitchen.

Standing, he was not especially tall, but long-limbed, and he moved languidly through the room with a slack bored face. This time, the bathrobe flailed open to reveal plaid pajamas. He did not look toward the piano, where Gretchen sat playing "Devil's Curtsy." But on his way back from the kitchen he paused by the stool, waved the butt end of an unopened Schweppes bottle at her, and said, "You again."

She glanced up at him and felt herself blushing. He grinned. Even with the mottled skin—grayish pink today, feverish, maybe?—he was the first person whom she wanted simultaneously to stare at and look away from. Fixing her eyes on the shaved-off part of his head made her feel less nervous.

"Ah, you're into scars? You might also be interested to know that, due to youthful indiscretion"—he shook his head dramatically and rolled his eyes upward—"I have a plate in my head that's set off metal detectors in airports all over the world. Luckily that didn't stop me from getting into Juilliard."

"You didn't go to Juilliard," Miss Grant exclaimed in an earnest, worried voice. "I did."

He laughed hysterically.

Miss Grant scowled now. Sighed. "We're in the middle of something here."

"Hmm. In the middle of something," he said, mocking her affected accent—nearly the opposite of his own soft drawl—and tapping his fingers across the piano top. "Everyone's in the middle of *something*, May." He looked past her and winked at Gretchen. "But it's rude to say so." Without another word, he turned away and padded slowly down the hall, the belt of his robe trailing behind him. Miss Grant looked flustered. The eye began to twitch.

Perhaps she noticed that Gretchen trembled too, for she was now offering her a cup of tea. Gretchen accepted.

Miss Grant boiled the water in a red-and-silver teakettle and gave Gretchen permission to select any mug she wanted from the shelf. Gretchen had never been invited to have tea (or even a drink of water) before. There were all kinds of mugs, some simple and modern-looking, some rustic and handmade, a few real dainty teacups with saucers. Gretchen selected a blue-and-white teacup. Miss Grant placed three tea bags in a jade teapot and poured water from the kettle into it. They sat at a little square table in front of the window. Miss Grant leaned forward, toward Gretchen, with her elbows propped on the table, and said that the way Gretchen had just played "Devil's Curtsy" interested her. As a beginner, she herself had played it "indolently," as Gretchen did, and though the music said to play it another way, she preferred *their* way. Gretchen had not meant to play it any particular way—did not understand the meaning of the word "indolent"; perhaps it was another piano term she'd failed to memorize. But still she had pleased Miss Grant; she half-smiled and mumbled in agreement. A silence followed. Then a long stare from Miss Grant, a flicker of her lipsticked smile and her white fingers slipping through the black tips of her hair. Now she frowned severely. She began to speak of her grandparents, whom she'd lived with in this house, when she was Gretchen's age. She did not touch her tea but wrapped the fingers of one hand around her cup. She said that her grandmother played every morning and night. You woke to music and you fell asleep to music. Sometimes you woke up in the middle of the night thinking you heard a song until you got to the piano and saw that no one was there. That happened still. Which led Miss Grant to the theory that you did not create music but let it pass through you. "An instrument is simply a tool. I can feel all of the music my grandmother played still in the house. I think you can feel it too, Gretchen."

Gretchen nodded, though she felt nothing like that, didn't want to feel it. It was funny to realize that Miss Grant thought she was someone else. Miss Grant had never talked so much before, not like this. She stared intensely at Gretchen, her eyes full of light.

"At Juilliard, I had a fiancé named Gregory."

Miss Grant told Gretchen that both she and Gregory had recitals in the same week. They both ended up wanting to play the same concerto. Gregory always worried that she played better than him, and he asked her if she would play something else, since he was a third-year student and she a first. She said no. He told her if she played the concerto, he did not want to see her anymore.

"I played it, Gretchen. I played it perfectly." There was a long pause—the words had an air of triumph—and finally she sipped from her tea. The fingers of her other hand played nervously across the tabletop, and for no particular reason, Gretchen feared Miss Grant would try to take her hand. Perhaps she would cry. She watched Gretchen with wet expectant eyes, the spell broken by the creak of the door and the appearance of Fiona Xiu. A pair of leather sandals with braided straps snaked around her ankles. She smacked on a wad of blue gum.

Miss Grant started and her tea sloshed over the rim of her cup. She offered Fiona a cup, which she declined, and got up to rinse out the teapot. Fiona joined Gretchen at the table while Miss Grant stepped outside.

Fiona studied the fancy teacups on the table, and glanced over at the cup-laden shelf. She had a vivacious, moon-shaped face and black eyebrows plucked in perfect tapering arches.

"That's a fuckload of cups."

Gretchen nodded. She watched Fiona push back the cuticle of her index finger, and as nonchalantly as possible asked Fiona if she'd noticed Miss Grant's brother living in the back. Fiona said that she had. "He, like, came out one day in the middle of my lesson and said something like 'She's been marked from the start.' And then he pointed to her feet and said one of them was bigger than the other. He's a nut." She picked up Gretchen's teacup and examined its blue-and-white arabesques. "He was trying to rattle her. I think. He's cute for an old guy. Or, he would be if the side of his head wasn't fucked up." Fiona took a sip from Gretchen's cup. She did not hand it back.

The screen creaked, and Miss Grant came back into the kitchen. Gretchen's mother had pulled up, she said. Gretchen paused for a moment to stare at Miss Grant's feet. One foot was in fact at least a size larger than the other.

III

"Are you still loving the piano?" her mother liked to say, leaning in the doorway, sometimes lightly rapping her nails against the piano's headboard, her smile forgiving Gretchen for not wanting to talk with her about boys or secret feelings, about any of the things that mattered; her eyes catching Gretchen's father's as he passed by the door and stopped to stand by her, their bodies closing the space between inside and out.

"Yeah. Sure."

"Can you play Moonlight Sonata?" her father would ask, in a tone that suggested he did not remember asking twice before. Many nights since her parents had begun sleeping apart she had, jolted and sweaty from some nightmare she couldn't remember, lingered by the door to the guest room, now her father's door, to catch him talking in his sleep. But during these times she had heard nothing but his breath.

"I've always thought it was the most beautiful piece of music," he went on.

"Not yet. But I will," she promised. "Probably," she began to retract.

No.

The words felt oddly disconnected from her, like lies. Or like their faces, desperate for affection she could not give them, leaning toward her. She did not think, *I am lying.* She did not think in reply to her father, *Even this little thing I can't do for you.* But afterward this was what she felt.

IV

Yes, Miss Grant had moods. Now she scrutinized the theory workbook pages she'd assigned last lesson. She stabbed at the pages with her red pencil, and from time to time looked up to glare at Gretchen, who was ambling through her scales while Miss Grant marked. Did she stab harder at the pages than usual? Did Gretchen imagine this?

Gretchen hadn't practiced her prescribed schedule (she rarely did), though she convincingly executed simple melodies or scales whenever her parents passed by the room.

During the last few lessons, she'd halfway opened the door to Miss Grant's house—Miss Grant gave her permission to let herself in at lesson time—so that her mother would see and pull down the drive. And then she'd shut the door and stay outside on the stoop, hurriedly filling in the pages. But today— of all days—because Miss Grant stood outside smoking, she had had no choice but to hand over the half-finished assignment.

Part of her wanted Miss Grant to yell at her, to tell her she'd done a terrible job. "You're bad and stupid," she imagined Miss Grant saying, as Gretchen's mother, who never called her names, had once said to her in a dream. *No*, she thought, when Miss Grant stopped suddenly, looked right at her with a steely expression. Miss Grant looked down again, went on with her marking. She spent a great deal of time scrawling notes that Gretchen never read. No sounds touched the air, none but the scrape of the pencil tip.

They'd gone through a third of the lesson time and Wesley had not yet appeared. And how could Gretchen possibly go after him, now that Miss Grant knew?

Outside the yard looked hot and still. Nothing moved, not even the Easter eggs, the strings of which you couldn't see, so that in quick glances they looked like colors strung from the air. Clouds shifted. The yard went gray with shadow. Bright and then gray again.

Wesley. Wesley. Wesley. She tried to summon him with her thoughts. She brushed a hand against the silken hem of her dress.

"Do your parents know about this?"

Gretchen started. Her heart raced violently.

"I mean, you're obviously not taking your workbook seriously. I didn't say anything before because I thought the notes were enough. Obviously they're not."

V

The day Miss Grant's brother had fallen in love with her—the day after school let out for the summer—Gretchen had found a note on Miss Grant's door. It said that she'd had "a minor emergency" and misplaced their number, and went on and on about how "very very sorry" she was for their "inconvenience." Because her mother usually lingered in the driveway until she stepped inside, Gretchen shoved the note in her pocket and tried the door. It was unlocked. She waved to her mother and her mother waved back, the car already moving in reverse. She stepped inside.

The house was dim and silent with Miss Grant's absence, the blinds in the kitchen and piano room left closed. Gretchen had shaved her legs that morning and the silk of her dress rustled soft and cool and fresh against her legs as she walked. It was the first time she'd worn it—a new dress her mother had bought her for church, its silk printed with overlapping circles of milky rose, turquoise, ginger, and gold. Her mother had said it looked "too dressy" to wear to lessons, but she had waited until the last minute to change into it because she knew that her mother would not send her back to her room for fear of being late. Wearing the dress for *him* made her feel formal, especially feminine, as if in it she accepted a new code of behavior, and she paused at his door, wondering if she should knock this time. But what if he didn't answer?

She slowly turned the knob and let herself in.

He lay on his bed reading a thick black hardcover. He had his arm propped up on the comforter, which had been half rolled, half scrunched up, and the sheets were twisted away from the bed, so that some of the mattress showed. He did not seem so much surprised as amused to see her standing in his doorway. The room smelled a mix of sourness and tomato soup. The blinds were drawn; light came only from the two small lamps placed at either side of the bed. In the corner of the room she could see a case of trophies, the silver and gold of the trophy figures faintly limned. "She got called in. Didn't she leave you a note?" he said.

"Called in by who?"

"By *whom*." He carefully folded down the top right corner of the page he was on and closed the book. Last time his face had looked happy and silly, but now it looked disarmingly serious, so that he looked more like a real sick person. "She's just not here, all right?"

"My mom's already driven away."

"Well you're going to have to call her."

"She's out shopping. It's too far to go back home. And I don't know which stores," she said, anticipating what might follow. To prove that she was there to stay, she pulled the wooden chair from the desk in the corner and turned it to face the bed, then sat. After watching her for a minute he sat up. He sighed, reopened the book, shut it, and with a flick of his bony wrist flung it just past the trophy case. It was a heavy book and Gretchen started at the sound of it smacking the wall. "I hate that book," he said, laughing, like it had been a joke. For a minute she was afraid. But then he smiled sweetly and turned toward her. "May says you have a natural touch, but that you don't practice much. She says you could be very good though."

"I hate playing piano," Gretchen said. What she meant to say, to clarify, was that she wasn't at all like Miss Grant.

"Don't tell May that. She'll die. She loves the piano. She lives for the piano, I think." He said this in a confusing way, contempt in his voice, but his eyes showing something softer.

Gretchen snickered, liking the sudden intimacy brought about by criticizing her teacher with him. "She loves the piano like . . . like you'd love a person."

"Yes. That's it exactly. There's nothing more disgusting than misplaced affection. Especially regarding pianos. *Eew*." He grimaced in an exaggerated way that made her smile. He smiled back. "You're a mean girl. Pardon, a mean young *woman*. How old are you anyway? No . . . wait," he said, before she could answer. "I'll guess."

"What do you guess?"

"I'm keeping it to myself." He crossed his legs at the ankles and folded his arms. "Don't know what we're going to do until your mother gets here."

But apparently he did. Because he reached into the drawer of his bedside table and brought out what Jamie would've referred to as a "dime bag." (She had never smoked pot with Jamie, but he'd described it and bragged about having it at parties.) Also from the drawer, he took a thin sheet of paper. He tore it, dropped some of the leaf bits on it, rolled it up and then ran his tongue across the edge of the roll. "Your dress reminds me of carnival grass," he said. "The colors. Have you ever been to Venice?"

"No."

"Well what about the flea market? I think they sell something like it there."

"Never been."

"Well where have you been, *Miss* . . . I don't even know your name."

She told him her name.

"Gretchen. Gretchen." Each time he pronounced it slowly and carefully, as if the name were unique. The sound of it caused gooseflesh to creep over her arms and legs. She babbled about visiting the Smithsonian in D.C. with school, and then about the condo her parents owned on Pawleys Island.

In the dimness of the room his eyes looked more bourbon than mint, and the lamps carved out smooth hollows beneath his cheekbones. A layer of fuzz now masked the part of his head that had been shaved before. You could hardly see the part where it dipped and swelled, and she both hoped and feared he was better. If he was well, she did not have to worry about his dying. But if he was no longer sick, she could not imagine him here, in his room. Here with her.

"The beach, hmm? So tell me, Gretchen, are you a one-piece or a two-piece girl?" He put the cigarette to his mouth, which was wide and narrow like Miss Grant's, but curvier around the edges. By the time she realized he was talking about bathing suits and opened her mouth to answer, he said, "Wait. Don't. I'll just guess."

"Are you keeping it to yourself again?"

He half laughed, half choked on an exhalation of smoke. Gretchen asked if she could have some of the pot, not because she wanted it so much as she wanted to climb up on the bed beside him. He shrugged his shoulders and she took this as a yes. She crawled onto the bed. She sat so that her shoulder touched his upper arm, which felt smaller than it should be, even under the thick cotton. He moved an inch away, so that they were no longer touching, and passed her the cigarette. "You have to hold it in for a minute," he said as she inhaled. Before she had fully breathed it in she choked a little. Her eyes watered but she smiled to show him she was okay. She wanted to say she knew more than he thought she knew. She knew about what to do. But he kept talking.

"It's all about a lack of imagination. Lack of the need for it. See, with the two-piece, especially of the thong variety, you can see almost *everything*. Nothing left to the imagination. You know everyone looks basically the same under their clothes but you don't *know*. And now you do. That's how it is now." He took another drag from the cigarette and passed it back to her. Their fingers momentarily brushed. She inhaled again, this time without choking, and held it in as he'd told her. Her eyes fixed on his bare knee, exposed by the part in the robe. She could not look away. Its down was almost the same color as his skin, its contour sharply curving, and it seemed secretly beautiful. "Another example," he went on, now gesturing elaborately with his other hand so that he appeared to be drawing in the air. "I've seen the inside of my head. It's just an organ, like a kidney, and you expect that but you don't. You've seen pictures at school, haven't you?" She nodded. "I wish I hadn't seen it. I'd have imagined it as light. Colors. At least *colorful*. I'd like to think the inside of my head looks like your dress."

She fingered the hem of the silk, the part that fell across the middle of her shin. He leaned toward her, just a little, so that his arm rubbed against her shoulder.

"I wore it for you."

She kept playing with the hem of her dress while he watched. You'd have thought she was performing magic, the way he watched. She wanted him to kiss her. (Jamie had always started by kissing her shoulder, or her ear, before her lips.) Finally, he pressed his palm to the side of the lower part of her back and said that her kidney was there, in case she hadn't known. His breath smelled smoky and stale, but there was that other scent, the scent of his skin suffusing the air around them. With his own long wiry fingers, perhaps the part of him that most resembled Miss Grant, he trapped Gretchen's hand and the silk it held. He pressed his face into her hair, murmuring, *God, but I love her,* as if announcing his feelings for Gretchen to a third party. And pressed his dry lips to her temple.

Suddenly he pulled away. In a different, more authoritative tone he announced that her mother would soon arrive. He said she should go to the bathroom in the hall and find the mouthwash. Then, he said, she should spray her clothes and hair with air freshener.

She sat for a minute, dumbly staring at his handsome face.

"Leave, I said." He sounded angry now and she rose too quickly. Dizzy, with splotches of blackness clouding her vision, she climbed off the bed and gently shut the door behind her. When she cracked the door and looked back, he lay on his side, facing away from her. He was curled up into himself, quiet but breathing funny.

She had gone back only to see if he was all right.

But he had pulled her down into his smell, against his protruding ribs and the pale down of his chest. He had guided her hand between the folds of the robe and with the other hand she had touched the ruined part of his scalp. Beneath the robe his sex was surprisingly soft, and after a moment she knew that what he wanted her to make happen with her hand would not. And that was when Miss Grant came in. Her mouth dropped open so that Gretchen expected her to scream, but no sound came out.

Gretchen did not hear her yelling until she was almost out of the house. The voice, which she'd never really heard raised, sounded shrill and broken, almost like crying. She wanted to stop and listen. Wanted to see Miss Grant's face twisted with a feeling that didn't come from the piano. Wanted Wesley to declare his love for Gretchen to another human being. But for fear that Miss Grant might suddenly decide to come after her, she ran down to the foot of the drive, to hide behind the trees until she saw her mother's car.

VI

"It's correct, but you're not playing it like you *could* play it."

Gretchen again began the piece. Her fingers moved clumsily over the keys because she was also looking out the window. The weather changed so quickly. A moment ago it had been hot and still, and now the wind had picked up. The sky cast the yard a grayer shade of green, and the chartreuse of the weeds faded. The plastic Easter eggs batted violently, erratically, the cord of the purple tangling with the cord of the orange.

The lesson was almost over and he had not appeared. She had thought of him all week. His laughter and kiss and scent. The way he said her name.

Thunder boomed in the distance and in mimicry she hit the B, C, and D at once. Miss Grant sighed. "Ignore the weather. Focus," she said. Her lips looked a brighter red, her skin a brighter white without the sun streaming through the window—Snow White with a long beaked nose and kohled eyes. The rain began with one, two isolated drops against the windowpane, and then poured down in heavy sheets. Less than a minute later, hail rattled across the roof. Gretchen stopped playing and both of them stared out the window now, hypnotized.

The phone rang, and Miss Grant went into the kitchen. *Yes, yes, of course that would be all right.* "Your father says they're stuck halfway across town and the traffic is barely moving," she called to Gretchen.

"Would you like to get a head start on the new one?" she said, strolling back into the piano room.

Gretchen said she had a headache and briskly gathered together the sheets of her music. She hoped that Miss Grant would leave her alone. Then she would be able to go to Wesley's room.

"You can sit there, then." Miss Grant gestured to the peach sofa. Gretchen collected her books, moved toward the sofa. She glanced back to see that Miss Grant was not going anywhere; she had slid onto the piano stool. Defeated, a little panicked by the mix of his nearness and unavailability, Gretchen dropped onto the lumpy cushions of the sofa.

The piece was silly, a simple, playful waltz that Miss Grant played lazily, as if she were half asleep. While she was playing, Fiona Xiu came in with her bag. Miss Grant, under the spell of the music, did not acknowledge her. Fiona looked from Gretchen to Miss Grant, to Gretchen again, and the girls exchanged a smirk. Fiona sat by Gretchen on the couch. She sat close and let her shoulder fall into Gretchen's, as if they were good friends, and on another day, this kind of closeness might have been enough. Her and Fiona sinking into friendship as they sank into the cushions, staying up late to watch movies and disdaining one another's parents, trying on each other's clothes and wandering around the mall to get eyed by clusters of guys. But Gretchen felt beyond all this now, and for some reason—but why? maybe because of the slight air of cunning, the shoes, her lazy grace—she suspected Fiona beyond it too. And so Gretchen wanted to tell Fiona all about her love for Miss Grant's brother, but held back due to her sense of Fiona's physical superiority; the animal sense of knowing that the girl beside you could take what you had. This drew a wall between them.

The music had changed now. It sounded slow but certain, like flowing water, becoming gradually faster, complicated, rushing, now erupting, so that Miss Grant's fingers seemed to flit over the entire keyboard in wild staccato. She played passively, a showy, indifferent clatter that mimicked the sound of hail on the roof. Did Gretchen slide away from Fiona, or Fiona from Gretchen? Because they now had a space between them. The space was also the music. The music, lovely and terrible and brutal, sounded like none she had heard. It sounded like Miss Grant's fingers digging into Gretchen's shoulders, sounded like the intensity in her eyes. Her lips murmured unintelligible sounds in the way Gretchen, before she knew better, had once imagined her father's lips moving in his sleep. *This is the way you must play always.*

When the electricity went out, Miss Grant continued to play. In the blue dimness, she saw Miss Grant's dark figure swaying over the keys. Now the song slowed, and Miss Grant bent over the keys, as if trying to get closer to the song. Closer, closer, Gretchen felt herself drawing closer too.

But it was gross, the angle of Miss Grant's bent back, and when Gretchen thought of this the music released her. Quietly, she rose from the couch. Miss Grant did not look away from the keys.

The hall looked as it might have looked at night, dark and blank, with a thicker stale-sweet smell. The pounding of the hail had slowed to a light patter. When she opened the door, she saw that the bed had been carefully made. The room was empty. It smelled of Lysol. The electricity had switched back on, and the light from the hall illuminated the pale bedspread, reflected in the glass of the trophy case. She knew that he had died. He had died, and the thing between them would be like a dream now. The room grew hazy. She sank down to the floor and propped her back against the side of the bed frame.

She did not know how long she'd been sitting there when Miss Grant walked in.

"He's gone to stay somewhere else, Gretchen."

"Gone where?"

Sometime between now and the time she'd entered the room, the hail had stopped and the purple sky had turned a dingy blue. She saw this in the slits of the blinds as she rose to stand. Miss Grant did not step all of the way in. She leaned against the doorframe and played with the brass doorknob. "It's best for him to stay somewhere else." She cleared her throat. "What he did to you was . . . I would be happy to talk to your parents if . . ." She looked down and let her messy dyed hair hide her face.

Then Gretchen was crying with Miss Grant's arm around her. The nape of Gretchen's neck touched the damp armpit of Miss Grant's silk shirt and they moved out of the room in this way, down the hall. In the piano room, Fiona Xiu still sat on the peach sofa with her books. Her eyes widened, and her arched brows shot up. She studied both of them curiously. Gretchen jerked away from Miss Grant and ran into the kitchen, out the back door.

Outside, her father's car had just begun to pull up the long curving drive. She could see her parents' faces blurred by the fogged-over windshield. She wiped her face with the side of her arm. She forced a calm over herself. Behind her the screen creaked, and Fiona appeared.

"You left them on the couch."

Gretchen accepted the books. She felt Fiona watching as she opened the car door and settled in the seat. Fiona watched still as they backed down the drive. The rain had stopped but ran off from the roof and fell like a clear, shiny curtain before Fiona's curious face.

THE NEGATIVE EFFECTS OF HOMESCHOOLING

My mom got the mink from a woman who used to be a man. It was a long thick coat that came almost to her knees, and when she wore it she looked half her usual size and not her age, like a little girl wearing something her parents said she'd grow into. Its fur was white and shot with umber streaks. The streaks turned lighter at their edges, broken up with white like streaks of dry-brushed watercolor. Then, I knew all about dry-brush watercolor because I was into Andrew Wyeth. I'd committed acts of passion while staring at a book of *The Helga Pictures*, which I'd had to steal from the library because I was sixteen and lonely, and all the desire and shame and the layers of desire, of which I've only recently become aware—Wyeth's desire for Helga, my desire for Helga, my desire for Wyeth's desire for Helga—had warped my brain, so that my imagination tried to turn half the things I saw into his paintings. But this is beside the point. This time, the coat really did look like that.

And my mom was already thirty-five and wouldn't grow into anything, which made the coat look sad rather than hopeful. But I grew all the time, so much that sometimes I couldn't remember what I'd looked like the month before. Walking with her, thinking this, I didn't even notice the guy coming toward us until he darted past me. He wore ratty clothes, like a bum, but had the clean young face of a college student. Before I could figure out what was happening he threw a cup of soda at her. "Death is not fashion," he yelled, and ran through the leafless clusters of elms and across the long stretch of grass toward the road. I yelled out, "Fuck you," and my mom acted more upset about this than his throwing the drink. She said, "Why do you have to use that kind of language?" And I said, "It's just a word." *Just a word*, she said in her ironic voice. She flipped up the edge of her mink, the part stained with soda, and gave this trembling frown, like she was trying not to cry.

"Take it off and take mine," I said. "It looks weird on you anyway and the spot's gonna make you crazy."

What I meant was that she had OCD and usually couldn't stand wearing clothes with even the smallest stain on them. But she just wrapped the mink tighter around her waist and glared at me.

To soften her, I said, "You look nice," which must have sounded stupid coming from me because I never said things like that to my mother. But she did look nice, if you didn't count the fur. Beneath it she wore a fitted black dress, and her hair, usually pulled back in a ponytail, hung in dark waves around her face. She looked better than most women her age, like one of those thirty-five-year-old women who look like only slightly rumpled versions of their twenty-five-year-old selves. The guys on my soccer team said, "How can you stand your mom looking so hot?" And I said, "The way you stand looking at your ass-face in the mirror." Inside I felt proud and sick at the same time.

We were in Connecticut, walking through this big green square in the middle of the town Charlene had moved to, going to the church where Charlene's funeral would be held. We had come all the way from South Carolina, even though Mom hadn't talked to Charlene in nearly a year. In addition to paying her respects, Mom also meant to represent Charlene's great-uncle, a sickly old guy from our church, who couldn't travel. My father was an elder at the church and got out of going because this other elder was in critical condition at the hospital. So I had to go so my mom wouldn't be alone.

The sky was dirty white with only a tinge of blue. As we walked, I could see my breath in the air and feel the frosted-over grass crunch beneath my feet whenever I wandered off the pavement. Earlier that morning, while I was waiting in the lobby for my mom to finish getting ready, I'd read the front of the paper in the paper-box and saw something up in the corner about an animal rights protest today, on the green. And there they were: way far in the distance a group of people carrying huge signs with pictures of cows and chickens and rabbits that read "Compassion," and buzzing with words I couldn't make out. They faced the other direction and the whole time we walked by I prayed in my head that none of them would turn, or stray from the group like their friend had, and see my mom's coat, the soda-stained fur of which had already begun to smell doggish. I put my arm in hers to hurry her along and she gave me this startled look, probably thinking I'd decided to be a gentleman. As we walked she went limp and leaned into my shoulder. She let me lead her along until her heel got caught in a ridge in the sidewalk, and then she pulled away and wiggled her tiny foot back in her shoe. She looked up at me like *I'd* tripped her, and made a sour face. "You're not wearing a tie," she snapped. I hadn't been wearing it the whole time—not since the cab *or* the hotel—but she hadn't said a word about it.

"You didn't say to wear it."

"I didn't *say* to wear your loafers, Conner. I didn't *say* to brush your teeth or put on your deodorant. It's a *funeral*."

"I didn't. I didn't put on my deodorant."

Then we walked not touching. The church was in the center of the green. It had a huge steeple that climbed far above all of the treetops, long white columns, and carvings around a pair of doors more than twice my height. Inside, organ pipes ran all along the top of the rear wall. There were two chandeliers, one of them dripping with crystals, and stained-glass windows with pictures of pilgrim-looking people in blue and purple and gold robes, their faces pale with light. The pews didn't look full, but they didn't look empty, either. We sat in the middle, where you could just see the top of the closed casket and the violet and white flowers spilling over it. My mom draped her mink over the top of our pew so that the stained part faced the opposite direction, and stroked a clean patch of its fur, like it was still alive. When the organ started up I felt the vibrations of its notes through my feet and I saw that my mom had changed—that the skin beneath her eyes looked papery, with nets of purple veins stretching just beneath the surface. A shiver went up my spine and I felt all spiritual and corny. Sweat began to trickle down my armpits and I wished I hadn't forgotten the deodorant.

In the hotel my mom had told me that Charlene attended this church. But this church looked nothing like the church she went to with us in South Carolina. There, we sat in fold-out chairs, in a messy circle. We didn't have a preacher because it was a liberal kind of church my father founded. Everyone just stood up and said things or read things from the Bible, whatever they wanted. No organ. No stained glass. No chandeliers. No robes like the preacher who now fumbled at the altar with his papers wore, because my dad thought fancy churches and organs and robes tricked people. "Pretentious ceremonial garb," he called it.

I kept looking around me, trying to find the other people pretending to be a sex they weren't. Imagining them everywhere, men trying to trick me into thinking they were women, and women pretending to be men, I hadn't even been able to sleep on the plane. But the people around us looked normal enough, just somber-looking people in funeral clothes. "Does Charlene stand for Charles?" I asked Mom.

"That's a very rude question."

"Rude how?"

"This is one of my closest friends, do you understand?" She kept changing on me. Now pink rimmed her eyes and her pale skin looked drained to the color of bone. Andrew Wyeth could have really made something of her.

"You haven't even talked to her in forever."

No answer. The organ paused and started up again. The sound went up inside of me and I tried to push it out but I couldn't and I thought that my father was right: I was being tricked into *something*. Was Charlene wearing a suit or dress inside her coffin? When I whispered this to my mom, she asked if I'd please wait for her outside. It wasn't really a question, though I think she'd have let me stay if I promised to behave. But I wanted to smoke anyway, so I just did what she said. I figured I'd make it up to her later.

Outside, I stood on the cement steps and lit a clove. I'd bought them from one of the church kids who had his own car. My mom hated that I smoked, but she couldn't do much about it except put pamphlets with pictures of black abscessed lungs on my desk and throw my packs away if she found them in my pockets when she did the laundry. Holding a clove, I felt philosophical. The trail of smoke resembled the life process. It started very small, just like humans started, and then it got fatter and less defined, like most of my older relatives, and then it just disappeared. Poof. Of course Charlene had not gotten fatter and less defined but thinner. She was anorexic. It had something to do with her dying. Maybe because she was so tall, plus really a man, she could only get smaller like a woman by narrowing herself.

The cement was freezing my feet but also stimulating my thoughts. Standing there, I thought how warm and beautiful and perfect it was in Charlene's church and wondered how it must have felt to go there every Sunday and feel the vibrations of the music against the soles of your feet. I could go back in, but what was the point? At home I'd have to keep going to my parents' church, where I always felt edgy or confused or just bored.

Even though no one could hear me, I used some profanity and pictured my mother, how much it would piss her off.

Even before she moved, Charlene had stopped coming to our house because of how I glared at her. When she and my mom sat at the dinner table sipping coffee, I brought my schoolwork into the living room—just outside the line where the living room stopped and the dining room began—so I could lie on the floor and stare until she looked over. When she did, I glared at her. She would start stirring her coffee and moving her hands faster than usual, feathering her crunchy blond hair. She would cross and uncross her legs, which bugged me because they looked like a real woman's legs, and make an excuse to go. My mom never noticed me glaring because talking to Charlene made her all dreamy and reflective; she thought everything Charlene said was wise. Like when my mom got mad at me for swearing, Charlene would say, *It's okay, June, it's just an assertion of his masculinity*, and smile in this knowing way that made my mom laugh.

The last time she came over I followed her to the bathroom. In the hall, I said, "I saw you in my mom's room that time. Messing with her stuff." What she knew I meant was that I'd once seen her try on one of my mother's dresses when she thought she had my mother's room to herself. It was during a dinner party. Her gaunt face, all broad bones and deep hollows and wide raisin-colored lips, fell in on itself, and just as quickly turned up into this tight smile. She said, "How?" And I said, "How what?" And she said if what I said actually happened, then how did I see it?

"Through the window." Not quite the truth.

"Oh, I see. This is your idea of a joke, Conner? Because the party didn't start until seven-thirty. Your mother would have closed the blinds by then." This was true. The blinds went up at seven every morning, and down at seven in the evening, no matter the season or what it looked like outside. I was screwed—I didn't want to explain how I'd really seen her—and I didn't know what else to say. I just stood there. She raised her eyebrows like she'd said something smart and slammed the bathroom door behind her.

The smell of her perfume stayed in the hall. She wore White Shoulders, like my great-aunt Martha, who's about a hundred years old and wears her overcoat inside, even in the middle of summer.

———

I don't know when exactly she gave my mom the mink, but I can guess. Mom went out twice, alone, the week before Charlene moved, and then, a few days later, I heard my dad complaining in my parents' bedroom, "It takes up half the closet, June." When I wandered in he was standing in his boxers and glaring into the closet, at the mink wrapped in plastic. My mom sat at the dresser brushing her hair. "Don't you see how my suits are getting mussed by it, June? Will you just turn around for a minute?"

Probably Charlene died thinking I was a jerk, but she did creep me out, and I did have a lot going on then. For example, I had hard-ons ten or twelve times a day. I'd either just jerked off or needed to jerk off, or hoped at least a few hours would pass before I had to jerk off again. I disgusted myself. Yet being me had become significantly more interesting. Where as I once sat in my room bored, playing computer games or drawing, I could now look at a picture of Helga and feel entertained.

As I said, I do not approve of stealing. It's just that my mom took me to the library sometimes, and while she looked for biographies I looked at art books. You see a lot of naked women in the art books, but none of them look quite like Helga. There's this one picture where she's got her arms folded beneath her breasts and one breast hangs over her hand while the nipple of the other presses into the other hand; and you don't get this—this sense of the weight of it, the breast, I mean—in most of the other art books. And then, because there are all these watercolors and sketches that Wyeth did of her before the major paintings, you've got this ghost Helga. The ghost Helga is slippery, like maybe she's lying in space with nothing beneath her, or maybe she disappears halfway across the page, into a patch of fleshy watercolor; but too there's her breasts with the shadows beneath them, and her belly poking out, round and smooth.

You can almost feel it, the weight of that breast on her hand.

In one painting there is only Helga's body in a field of soft black. Her hair is golden, her body all white, as if glowing from the inside, the faintest blush on her lips and cheeks. Her hair curls against her bare shoulder. Her face is turned away from you. Around her neck she wears a cord of black velvet that disappears into the black around her. Also you can see her pubes.

And so I put it in my satchel, the book. We walked out of the library and the alarm went off, but the library clerk figured she hadn't desensitized my mom's books correctly. If I'd have gotten caught I had an excuse planned: one of the scruffy unemployed guys who camped out in the magazine section had put the book in my bag. My mom would believe this. "Stay away from those men," she always said to me.

But I didn't get caught. I didn't even feel *that* bad, honestly. Honestly I blamed Mom for my stealing Helga. Half of me wanted that alarm to go off, just to see her face when they took the book out of my bag. Just to see her flip through the pages.

Understand that because she homeschooled me, my exposure to real women was seriously limited. I saw women only at church. Though, like I said, we went to a progressive church, our women looked the opposite of progressive to me: big glasses and no makeup, long skirts and cropped haircuts. You couldn't imagine any of them posing naked. You couldn't imagine any of them going off with Andrew Wyeth, alone into the woods. You couldn't even imagine wanting to take one into the woods. But there were exceptions, which only created more problems for me: Mrs. Kapawski, Ally Kapawski, and Charlene (if you consider her a woman). Mrs. Kapawski was all blond and powdery and flushed pink in her cheeks. She had big breasts that kind of bounced when she walked and I wondered if Ally would grow them too. Ally looked like her except thin, fourteen, with darker blond hair the color of Helga's and eyes almost always dilated like someone was shining a flashlight in her face. The face itself looked perpetually snobby, bored. Looking at it made me wild with desire, almost as much as looking at Helga did.

I watched Ally all during service, the congregation's words just noise, my heart racing almost as fast as it did at soccer practice. Sometimes I even tried to draw her on my devotional pamphlet, though the drawing never looked right, with the top of her head always trailing off the page. Afterward, while the adults had their coffee, I ran around with the other boys, in and out of the building around the parking lot. We ran and yelled like the whole place was a soccer field, but I never forgot she might be watching. Out on the lawn, she had her own thing going on. She made up plays for the other girls to act in. If you went close enough to hear the basic plot, you'd hear something about a suicide, or an affair. Apparently Mrs. Kapawski watched the soaps. Anyway, Ally did most of the acting, throwing out her arms and fake-weeping (it was the only time she looked fully awake), and the other girls circled around her, pretending to be sisters and maids, whatever. I made a habit of charging through the circle of girls whenever I saw a gap. Just running through to whoosh right past Ally while she acted.

Running so close that the breeze I made ruffled her blond hair. The other girls yelled at me. But except for flinching, Ally didn't even acknowledge me. Probably she didn't even care.

But like I said, I was homeschooled. Homeschooling elevated my maturity in some ways, like making me read above the level of most kids my age, but it also made me socially retarded. For example, one Sunday, when Ally looked really pretty in this mint-green sundress, I said, "Kind of stupid to wear a dress like that today, huh?" Because it was forty degrees outside and on the cusp of fall. "I mean, you must have wanted to wear it really badly to wear it today?" She rolled her eyes at me. Right after, Mrs. Kapawski came up beside her. She said she needed Ally to get her hand lotion from the car. I figured I'd follow her. I didn't have anything else to do anyway.

It was cloudy and gray that morning, but also gold. The gold shot through the gray and then it went away, reappeared in another part of the sky. This hill rose up against one side of the parking lot and from where I stood it framed Ally. The grass was dying, so the hill had different shades of brown and yellow in it, with a few bits of green. It could've been a Wyeth, except for all the stupid SUVs, and that Ally's dress looked too bright and new for a woman's in a Wyeth painting. I caught up to her; she cocked her head to look up at me, and then just faced straight ahead, like she didn't care. I followed her to her family's car, where she rifled through a bunch of junk in the back floorboard; who'd have thought Mrs. Kapawski—her hair always in place and her outfits so smooth and clean—would be such a slob, with empty drink cans and dirty sweaters and wrappers all over her floorboard? When Ally leaned into the backseat I pressed my side against hers and edged her in farther and she just let me, though she gave me this *What the hell are you doing?* look. I sat there for a minute staring straight ahead and said, "I wish we could just stay in here."

"We can't stay in here."

"Yeah, I know. That's why I said *wish*." For no reason I pushed down the headrest on the seat in front of me and it gave a loud click. "You never have any guys in your plays," I said. "In a real play people have to kiss."

"Why?"

"Haven't you read *Romeo and Juliet*? It's, like, the most famous play ever, and all about kissing. They aren't supposed to kiss, 'cause their families wouldn't approve, but they sneak away where no one can see them and, you know—"

"I *saw* the movie. It's okay with me."

"What's okay?"

"Okay to play it. I'm Juliet and you're—"

So I pressed my mouth against hers. She didn't kiss back but she didn't move away, either. I just pressed my lips to hers until I got embarrassed for not knowing what to do next (it was my first kiss, except for when my mom made me kiss Aunt Martha on the cheek and she turned her head really quick to make me kiss her lips instead) and then I got out of the car. She followed. She forgot the lotion. Of course Mrs. Kapawski noticed this, and also the fact that we'd come in from the parking lot together. After that, whenever I tried to be alone around Ally at church, Mrs. Kapawski came up and stood beside us. Her standing there made me feel like a creep, so that for a while I stopped hanging around Ally altogether.

Finally, one Sunday, the solution hit me. I walked over during one of Ally's plays and asked to join. She shrugged and looked over at her mom standing in front of the building.

Mrs. Kapawski was watching, but she didn't seem to care, I guess because of all the other girls around us. That was how I met Charlene. None of the other adults came out on the lawn—so long as they could see us from the lobby windows they didn't care what we did—but Charlene just wandered over that day and stood there.

Ally sat on the grass. In her hand she had an old film canister (probably from the pile of trash in her mother's car's floorboard), and pretended to pour pills out of it and lift them toward her mouth. I was the butler. This meant I got to stand close to her and pretend to be in her bedroom alone with her. I was supposed to interrupt her suicide to ask if she wanted tea. "Tea, ma'am?" I said. And Ally made a big show of hurriedly pouring the pills back into the canister. She put her fingers to her temples and grimaced. And then, in a calm polite voice, said, "Of course, Miles."

That was the end of it. Charlene applauded, but Ally and the other girls didn't notice because it wasn't a real clap. Just Charlene's two big hands fluttering quietly against each other. She'd come that morning with Mr. Harris, her great-uncle, an old stooped guy who always kept singing hymns a line or two after the rest of the church had finished. During service he'd leaned over and shouted in her ear, "You brought my mints?" She was very tall, all lines and edges, and her face, with its rough skin and crow's-feet and dark-mooned eyes, looked worn. Kind of haggard. Her leather skirt and stilettos looked flashy compared to the other churchwomen's clothes, but I figured she dressed like that to make up for her face, like some of the tiny wrinkled old ladies who wore new floral dresses each Sunday, or like the fat women who wore clunky jewelry and embroidered shirts.

She saw me notice her applauding, and winked. The girls had already started planning another play by the time she loped back toward the building.

So I had the problem of Ally—a girl I loved but could never be alone with—and then, for no reason, I ran into my room one day and tried to hurdle my desk chair. Instead of hurdling it, my legs got tangled in the top of it and I went down and fell on my knee this weird way, so it hurt whenever I bent it and the doctor said I had to sit out the season for soccer.

Then I didn't even get to leave the house in the afternoon, unless I went with my mother to the organic foods store or Vitawise, where she got all the chalky green tea and fish oil capsules she made me swallow in the morning. Or hung out with the other homeschooled kids in our network, who were socially retarded, with bad haircuts and board game obsessions. If my mom saw me "just sitting around" she gave me housework, like repapering all the drawers in the kitchen even though the old paper looked fine, and mixing vinegary homemade cleaning agents (which at least counted toward my chemistry requirement). Sometimes, if my dad stayed at work late, I just sat in the bathroom, on the rug, squishing bath beads over the shower drain and smelling the lavender. She hated me yelling stuff out about bodily functions— which I did if she came knocking—so she usually left me alone. I started hiding Helga in the guest towels and spending a lot of time there. For any amount of time I could study her body, white against the black. The weight of her breast against her hand. Her half drawn and vanishing into the white of the paper. She looked more real than real life. Always alone but also not alone, because the pictures were so full of want. Sometimes I didn't know where Wyeth's want ended and mine began.

Then, one night, I walked by my mom and dad's bedroom and heard my father tell my mother, "For so long, I've thought, I'll go through the motions and the faith will return." Pause. "But I don't *feel* anything, Carol." Then my mother said, "Conner is probably still up, Mike," and they lowered their voices. Just the evening before, he'd led a prayer at church, and I wondered if the prayer still counted for the rest of us if it didn't count for him.

Next thing I knew, my dad was gone all the time helping poor people get their electricity turned back on, or visiting people in the hospital, or working at the soup kitchen downtown. Which you'd think would be the opposite kind of behavior of someone who didn't *feel* anything about God. Half the time he came home after Mom and I had eaten dinner, and she had to warm his plate. If I got up in the middle of the night to use the bathroom I found him asleep in front of the TV.

Around that time Charlene showed up. The more my dad stayed out, the more she started coming over. At least when she came over my mom forgot about bothering me. Sometimes, from the kitchen, I watched them sitting there on the couch. Mostly they talked *on* and *on*, but once I found them just sitting there in silence, staring straight ahead, the afternoon light from the window flecking the mugs in their hands and their laps with gold. I didn't get the point of them sitting quiet like that. They might as well have been alone.

It pissed me off that she thought she was wise. *It's okay, June. It's just an assertion of his masculinity. Your husband isn't avoiding you. He's avoiding himself. No, I don't think you should get layers;*

your hair is too fine-textured. When she first came to the house
for coffee with my mom, I lay by the fireplace with my drawing
board propped against the ledge there. She knelt down and
said, "What are you drawing?" in a voice that reminded me
of sandpaper. She wore a short plaid skirt that made her legs
look too long, and a shiny blouse that rustled a little when she
moved her arm.

I told her I wasn't drawing anything particular. Just moving my pencil around to see what happened. This seemed to
make her happy.

"I do that too. I love to draw all the time." She brushed
some of the stiff blond curls from her cheek the way normal
women do. "But you know most people stop when they get
older. So it's important you continue to draw."

"For how long?" I'd gotten her point; I just wanted to be a
smart-ass.

"Well. As long as you live."

"What if my hands get mangled in an accident?"

She looked at me in this concerned way, like I might have
mental problems. The negative effects of homeschooling.

Then Mom called her over into the dining room, where
they had coffee and talked about how they were both reading
the biography of Zelda Fitzgerald. They said what a coinci-
dence this was, as the book had been out for "quite some time,"
and they'd both started reading it on practically the same
day. See, my mother read biographies all the time, and apparently Charlene did too (though you'd think someone like
her would have more exciting things to do, like go to trans
bars).

"Can you believe this part about her taking his material?"
Mom said, putting finger quotes over "taking."

"As if a *shared* experience could belong more to one person than another," said Charlene, grinning. "It's an adolescent viewpoint."

"But I understand the financial aspect of the situation. In a way, his viewpoint *was* worth more than hers."

"But I don't think it was about the money, June. No one wants to see his subject walk over to the easel and take up the paints, if you know what I mean."

Mom got all moon-eyed at this, like she thought Charlene spit diamonds. I thought I might throw up.

Then they started talking about their diaries. They called themselves "diarists."

"I've never met another true diarist," my mother said.

First I thought, WHAT IN THE WORLD did my mother have to put in a diary? All she did was give me assignments, wander around the house wiping things down, drink green tea, and go to stores. She never said anything to me about a diary; then Charlene's here thirty minutes and my mom is Anne Frank.

The next time Charlene came and brought *Breakfast at Tiffany's*. Before she put the DVD in the player, my mother said, "This is my *favorite* movie." She'd never mentioned this before either. While they watched the movie and held their little bowls of popcorn I rifled through my mother's bedside drawer and found the diary. It was a suede-covered book with unlined pages. Scared of what I might find, but also crazy with curiosity, I scanned the pages as fast as I could. But it didn't say anything. Just her schedule. *Walked this morning. Road wet from last night's rain. Conner continuing to struggle with geometry. Mike at soup kitchen again after work. Salmon and almond rice for dinner. Phoned Aunt Martha. Finished Jimmy Carter book.*

It went on like that for a bunch of pages. The most boring diary you could imagine. But then I saw her start saying C. instead of Conner. Then I realized C. didn't stand for Conner.

. . . *Had tea with C.* . . .

. . . *Read the Hughes biography with C.* . . .

For her latest entry, she hadn't written her schedule. She wrote only: *C. says that to accept your own malleability is the beginning of faith.*

There was nothing about me that day. Not even Dad. She'd kept up with our stupid schedules for months and months, and then stopped, just to put in some of Charlene's bullshit.

It made me so mad I started shaking. I slammed it back in the drawer the wrong side up (which is probably why she ended up moving it somewhere else), and went to my room to find a clean notebook. I would start my own diary and not mention her once. *Snobby gray eyes,* I wrote. Crossed out. Then, *I hate Charlene.* Then *shit* twice. I couldn't stand it. Suddenly I hated the whole idea of diaries and ripped up the page into tiny little pieces.

In the living room, they'd finished the movie. Charlene had my board with the sketch paper in her lap. She was showing off, drawing my mother. My mother sat very still and looked past Charlene, while Charlene's eyes flicked over her face, down at the page, over her face again. She had big long hands and made short rapid strokes and I wondered what it would feel like to draw a person like that, like your hand knew without a doubt what to do. I walked past them without saying anything, and as discreetly as possible glanced over to see my mother on the page, her slender nose and Chinese eyes and bangs falling over her forehead. Charlene's big hand, with its French manicure, danced all over the page, all over my mom's face. I went on into the kitchen. In the kitchen I drank really fast from a can of root beer. Passing back through the living room, I let out a great loud burp. Both of them stared at me. My mom glared but I pretended not to notice as I walked right through. "You're no Helga," I wanted to shout at her. But then I'd have had to explain myself.

How did I figure out Charlene was a man? It just hit me—that's the funny thing. One day I saw her at our dining room table sipping her coffee in the little china cups my mom set out for them, and maybe the light hit her wrong, or maybe she put her makeup on in a rush that day, or maybe it had to do with her sandpapery laugh or the way she touched my mother's wrist when they talked about their book.

"She's a man, isn't she? Like a drag queen?" I asked my mom that evening. We did, after all, have cable television.

My father cleared his throat. "Well, not exactly," he began. Though he didn't see Charlene much, as she usually came in the late afternoon when he volunteered at places, I could tell he didn't warm up to her like he warmed up to most people, patting their shoulders and grinning with his eyes lit up. "Well—" he started again. You never noticed how big he was until he started getting flustered and messing with his facial hair. "She's in a transitional phase. Technically she's—"

My mom cut in, "You're not to say anything like that around her, Conner. Understand?"

"I'm not an IDIOT. I know you don't go up to some man dressed like a woman and ask, ARE YOU A MAN? EVERY-BODY *KNOWS* THAT." She flinched, and I lowered my voice. "I just want to know if she's a man."

"Yes," Dad said. "Don't raise your voice at your mother." He looked down and picked at his beard. We ate in silence like that for about five minutes, and then everyone began talking like normal again, each describing our boring days.

If my mom knew what Charlene had done in her room—hold her earrings up to her ears, spray her perfume on her wrist, emerge from her closet wearing the lacy black dress she wore to holiday parties, and then gone back to the dining room like nothing had happened—would my mother be sitting in the church now, carrying around that stupid coat? Would I be standing in a strange town freezing my ass off? I'd thought about telling her a thousand times but the thought of saying the words made it seem more real, less like a bad dream.

The more I thought about it, the more impatient I got waiting for Charlene's funeral to end. I decided to take a walk. I went down the steps and back onto the sidewalk. The animal rights people were still there, but farther down the green, sitting on blankets while some guy paced and lectured. A couple of college-age kids were on a park bench on the other side of the sidewalk, making out. But when the woman brought her face away from the man's you could see they must have been almost sixty, just dressed like college kids with faded jeans and Birkenstocks clogs and J.Crew sweaters. At the end of the sidewalk, the main road. Buildings with columns and arches that looked hundreds of years old and nothing like the vinyl shacks that popped up overnight in my town. Across the street I saw a string of shops with brick walls. A café. I wanted to go in the café and buy a frappuccino but didn't know if I had time. Probably my mom would get pissed if she came out of the funeral and didn't see me, but so what?

When I opened the door to the coffee shop the warm air and smell of fried things made me feel sick, like someone breathing through his mouth in my face. The coffee shop wasn't the kind of place that sold frappuccinos and had bands and poetry readings, but rather like an old person's coffee shop, where people ate bacon. A foreign-looking middle-aged man sat on a stool behind the counter with a laptop computer. I fake-coughed so he'd look up.

"Yes?" He didn't have an accent, which disappointed me. I asked him for a frappuccino, just to see if they had them after all. They didn't, so I asked for a plain coffee.

"It'll stunt your growth." He laughed hard; I was already six-one.

"I'll chance it." It sounded like a pretty good comeback to me.

"Who died?" he said, raising his bushy eyebrows at my black blazer. He poured the coffee into a white mug that needed to go through the dishwasher again.

"My mom's friend Charlene. She was a guy who wanted to be a woman. Probably his name was Charles before he started dressing like a woman."

The man frowned. "What?" I'd offered too much information too soon. The negative effects of homeschooling.

"Never mind. How come nobody else is here?"

The man shrugged his shoulders.

Windows made up one whole wall of the place, so I sat by that wall, facing the street. Cars zipped up and down the street, but there were no actual bodies—no one on either side of the sidewalk. It was like me and the coffee shop man were entirely alone in the world. For a minute I imagined this scenario where we really had gotten separated from the rest of the world and could only communicate with it through the Internet on his laptop. He made me cook and clean the restaurant in exchange for Internet time.

He kept typing on his laptop, not looking up. He hadn't charged me for the coffee. In my head I named him Archibald, and in my head we conversed. "You have a secret, don't you?" Archibald said. I told him about Charlene in my mother's room. Archibald was appalled. He rubbed his tan forehead and slammed down the screen of the laptop. "But why haven't you told your mother all this time?" Archibald said. I drank some burnt coffee from my dirty mug and got reflective. I lit a clove even though I knew it wasn't allowed. Archibald didn't tell me to stop. It was really hot in the restaurant but my wet underarms definitely needed the cover of my jacket. *It's complicated*, I told him. I started explaining about the dinner party my mom had had before Charlene left.

A lot of families from church came, including the Kapawskis and Charlene. It was only a month after I'd kissed Ally and acted in her play, and when I saw her walk through the door in this fuzzy white sweater I had to look away to make my heart stop rushing. Charlene came in behind her, wearing the fur coat my mother would three weeks later come in wearing, saying Charlene had to move for a job. ("What job?" I asked Mom then. But she changed the subject.) Mom and Mrs. Kapawski made a big deal over the coat, oohing and ahhing. They rubbed the fur on Charlene's arm. "Is this real mink?" And blah blahh blah. Charlene: "My mother bought me this coat before she died. It's my favorite. It's just getting cold enough to wear it," blah blah blah. In my head I got a picture of this shriveled old lady in a low-lit room smelling of death, in bed hugging a big wrapped box. "Go on, be a woman. I'm okay with it now," she said, and passed the box to Charlene.

Like any other party, the kids finished eating my mom's lasagna in ten minutes, while the adults had only got started gorging themselves. Some of the teenagers played outside, at my basketball goal, and the Brenner twins let themselves into my room and started messing around with my computer. Everyone assumed Ally and I were playing with the others, but actually we went to my mom and dad's room. My mom already had the door shut, so I knew no one would think anything about me taking her in and shutting the door behind us. I said, "Want to sit on the bed?" And she said, "I don't care." So we did. I'd rather have taken her to my own room, to show her this halfway decent picture I'd sketched of the back of her head during church, and maybe get her to pose for me. But, anyway, because I knew the Brenner twins would run to their mom crying if I forced them out of my room, we had to hang out in my parents' room, with its beige walls, and beige bedspread, and pictures that didn't jump out at you, like the kind you buy in department stores. At least it was perfectly clean. My room kind of smelled like feet.

When we sat on the bed, we could see ourselves in the dresser mirror. I'd have laughed at this but she stayed serious, with her face blank, her arms folded in her lap. In the mirror I looked like a freak: my arms and legs had suddenly shot out half a foot that year and my clothes didn't fit right, no matter how often my mom got me new ones. I had some hair on my face but it grew in a patchy way. Actually, I had patches of hair all over my body in new places, like on my toes and ankles, in *other* places too. Did I smell like my bedroom? Did she notice how gross I was? A hairy chronic masturbator.

Because she looked beautiful. She wore a fuzzy white sweater. Her pale hair, which usually hung limp against her head, had static in it, rising up like a halo, and when I put my sweater sleeve against it strands of it stuck to me. She didn't seem to mind. I put my face close to hers and let my eyes flick over to the mirror to watch it happening. Her smooth pale skin looked brand-new. You could see the little blue veins beneath her eyes. You could imagine all the blood rushing through them while she sat there still. Helga had nothing on Ally sitting on my parents' bed with static in her hair.

She leaned away then, just a little (I saw it first in the mirror), and said, "You can't kiss me for real unless we're going to get married." She said it nonchalantly, like she might need to go to the bathroom.

"You want me to play like we're married?" She shook her head. "You mean, like, really married?" She nodded. "But people don't get married just to kiss," I said.

"If they want to kiss me, they do."

I watched us in the mirror, a snobby-faced girl in a white sweater with static hair. A dark gangly boy in navy-blue wool. I thought of the movie I'd seen on cable last year, about a rich man always trying to impress his cold beautiful wife. Probably it would be like that for us. We'd marry and I'd sell all my nude drawings of her to buy her stables and a Jacuzzi, a big mansion. She'd just roll her eyes. I'd build her a big greenhouse in the yard with every kind of tropical flower in it, from burn-your-eyes orange and blood-red to rich weepy blue, with a bunch of workers tending the flowers, like a little city. A fountain that poured into a pool you could swim in. With fish, if that didn't gross her out. But her face would stay slack and indifferent. My beautiful frigid wife. Like the man in the movie, I'd keep trying to impress her while she kept being frigid. Secretly she would hate me because I couldn't stand for her to kiss other men and wouldn't let her be an actress. Then, just like the woman in the movie, she'd kill me by throwing a plugged-in toaster into our Jacuzzi while I lay in there asleep. "I never liked his drawings," she'd say on TV, after my death.

"Okay. I'll marry you," I told her.

"You're not just saying it to kiss me?"

"No. I swear." I leaned my shoulder against hers. "You smell like baby powder."

"It's not baby powder. It's perfume that smells like baby powder."

"That's stupid." I said, and was instantly sorry. Ally moved her shoulder away. We looked sadder in the mirror but I would not let the sadness have me. I threw my arms around her and she didn't fight me. I put my tense lips on her soft calm ones. First I kept my eyes closed but then I opened them for a minute. She must've had hers open the whole time—snobby gray eyes wide and unseeing, like a blind person's. Something was wrong with her, something I couldn't put to words. I wanted to protect her from it.

Then I heard a warning sound: the loose floorboard in the hall that creaked when you walked across it. We got off the bed, me yanking her arm in the direction of the master bathroom. The doorknob rattled. When Charlene came in, Ally already sat against the wall, by the tub, not looking worried but simply waiting, like you might wait in a dentist's office. Maybe she made up plays all the time in her head when she wasn't acting. But my heart was exploding. I was sweating, looking out from the crack in the door.

My parents' room is shaped like an electrical cord socket, a big square that narrowly jutts out on one side, like a prong. My mom and dad's closets are in the prong part, the bathroom on the opposite side, on the other side of the wall from the dresser. The bathroom's French doors have little bumpers at the top and bottom so they don't knock together when they're closed, which leaves a decent-size gap running between them.

I saw Charlene from the side, staring at herself in the mirror, because she stood far enough back from it. Most of her disappeared from view, then reappeared holding a dangly pair of my mom's earrings—frankly, they looked like fishing lures—to her big man ears. Then she sprayed her wrists with my mom's perfume. She did it weirdly, by spraying the perfume into the air and then running her wrists through it. Then she went over into the walk-in closet. Of course I couldn't see into the closet; I saw only that she emerged from it in my mom's holiday dress. The lace pulled around her wide bony shoulders and the part of the dress that went out over my mom's hips bunched up around Charlene's long waist. That dress made her look more like a man than the things she usually wore, but she seemed to think it looked great, what with the way she kept smoothing her lap and turning in front of the mirror. She even gave this little laugh. I wanted to stop it right then, come out of the bathroom and tell her how stupid she looked, but it would have felt like walking in on her naked and having a conversation. I couldn't do it. I just stood there and tried to push her out with my mind. I looked back at Ally: she was messing with her cuticles. Did she even wonder why we were hiding in the bathroom? Did she know that Charlene was a man? The only stuff she ever seemed interested in was the stuff she made up in her head.

When I looked back, Charlene had already gone back into the closet. She came out in her own miniskirt and silk blouse. She left. It was like a dream. I couldn't kiss Ally now; I felt sick. I told her we needed to go outside to play with the other kids. "I don't care," she said. Outside, I darted away from her. I went into the cluster of magnolias in our backyard and puked up my lasagna all over the dead magnolia leaves. I sat there on the ground until the sickness went away. I found Ally by the basketball goal, sitting with Han, the only Korean girl at our church. She was telling Han that she had a part for her. Something about an affair between a husband and his family's exchange student. The other kids were running and screaming around our driveway, throwing a basketball back and forth, but she didn't notice. When the ball bounced right over her head, she didn't even bother to look up.

"So what'd your mother's friend die of?" This wasn't the pretend Archibald, but the real guy speaking to me as I returned my mug to the counter. He looked past me, out the window, where people suddenly filled the streets. They looked like they'd been there all along, strolling by in their scarves and coats. The wind had picked up and lifted the edges of a man's green scarf. A handful of dead leaves. A woman's long red hair.

"She was in this Jacuzzi and her husband threw a toaster in it."

"Really?" he said. I nodded and looked sad. He actually seemed to believe me. He mumbled, "Sorry," and went back to typing on his laptop.

It couldn't have been past four, but it looked much later, with the sky turning gray and some of the cars' headlights flicking on as they rolled down the street. The wind cut right through my jacket. I had sad thoughts: about how Ally had suddenly gotten acne all over, and oily hair, and how her snobby eyes made me feel sorry for her instead of turned on. About how my mom looked so bored when one of the church women came over to have coffee with her like Charlene had, and how she'd sometimes ask the woman the same questions, like "What are the kids up to today?" two or three times without remembering she'd already said it.

On the sidewalk running back through the green, groups of people in dark clothes strolled by. Probably they'd come from the funeral. Which meant the funeral had ended and my mom had probably started looking for me. I pictured her standing there in front of the church in her puffy coat, glaring and waiting. Maybe about to call the police.

But as I neared the church—which was lit up now, its windowpanes glowing in the grayness—I saw that she was talking to a group of people at the far side of the building, not even watching for me. Their clothes looked too bright for funeral clothes. Closer, I saw a few animal rights signs lying on the grass, two thin women with huge woven purses, and a guy in a green hoodie. One of the women gestured at my mom.

". . . a symbol of violence," she was saying to my mom. "How can you wear a symbol of violence and murder and not think about it?"

My mom had her arms folded around her, hugging herself.

"It was a gift—"

"A gift is given freely, not stolen," the woman said. "Those animals' lives were *stolen*."

"Do you know how mink fur is processed?" the man cut in. "They shove the minks into little cages, where they can barely move around. They can't get out of their cages, so they start biting themselves. Farmers try to kill them with hot engine exhaust, but it doesn't always work. Some of them wake up while they're being skinned." He pushed off his hood and stepped closer to my mom, so that his curly hair spilled over his collar. There was less than a foot between them and the clouds of their breath merged into each other. "It's easy: take it off and take a stand."

My mom didn't even see me. She just stood there holding herself and looking down at the ground like she was waiting for them to go away. I looked around for help, but there was no one there. We were off to the side of the building and if I went around the front, inside the church to get someone, I'd have to leave her alone.

"It was a gift. If the person who'd given it to me had known . . ." Her voice trailed off into silence. She fingered the place where the coat cinched at her waist.

"Be honest with yourself," he was almost shouting. He leaned forward and waved his hand at her. "There's no justification for—"

Then I was in the middle of them, up in his face, shoving him. He was a little shorter than me, but bigger around the chest and shoulders. Still, he went back pretty far and almost lost his balance. He shoved me back, but not hard enough to knock me down. Mom was yelling something but I ignored her and came at him again, my shoulder slamming into his chest, so that even through the padding of clothing and skin I could feel our bones collide. He slipped and fell on the sidewalk, his glasses falling off into the grass, the women instantly kneeling down beside him. "IT'S A GIFT FROM MY MOM'S DEAD BEST FRIEND," I screamed down at him. "CAN'T YOU TELL

SHE JUST CAME FROM A FUNERAL? HER BEST FRIEND IS DEAD." I couldn't stop myself. A salty taste filled my mouth, but I didn't feel like I was crying. Paper rustled beneath my feet. I kept screaming the same words, over and over, until I felt her hand press against my arm.

"Stop it, Conner. Please stop it," she said.

"He was going to hurt you."

I looked down at his bent figure, at the paper spread on the grass around him.

"No. He was trying to make me take one of his flyers."

The man looked up at me, his eyes small and blinking. The girls looked at me too. All of their faces showed more shock than anger. The rain had just begun to fall, and the wind rippled through the flyers, their white flashing beneath the light from the streetlamps.

"See, Conner?" Her eyes caught mine and held them. The wind lifted her hair from her face. "I'm okay now. *I'm okay.*"

VULNERABILITY

Men are afraid that women will laugh at them.
Women are afraid that men will kill them.

—MARGARET ATWOOD

I

Once I fell for my art dealer. He is a semi-famous gallery owner you might have heard of—the rumor that he discovered his love of art history as a bedridden teenager, recovering from a series of surgeries he won't specify, is true—and though I can't say his name here, I'll add that he's bearded, green-eyed, and tall, with a pale, nicely shaped head, and aware of whether or not you're watching his hands as he speaks. I think this is because when he was a teenager he believed no woman would ever desire him, and so even though lots of women like him now, part of him can't really accept it, and there he is having many brilliant thoughts about art and vision or business or insights into whatever it is you're telling him about, but all the while he's also paying attention to whether or not you're watching his hands.

As a teenager he read in one of those books socially awkward boys read in hopes of learning to relate to females that this is a sign that one human being desires another.

But I didn't know that then, about watching hands. And so I'll say that ten minutes into knowing him in person, I was. *I was.* (Though I can't say how much this had to do with his moving them a lot as he spoke, probably trying to get me to look at them.)

Sitting across from me in the restaurant where we met, with a very pleased, bright-eyed expression, he announced to me, "You're looking at my hands."

"Well, yes. I guess I am."

And he kept looking at me like that, in private delight, like something important had happened. I thought he might be crazy. I thought he was possibly the strangest person I'd ever met, and why were the buttons of his shirt unbuttoned so far down his chest? I could see a lot of chest hair (men where I lived in the South didn't do this with their shirts), and he was wearing, I think, a green shirt with thin pink stripes or a pink shirt with thin green stripes that was a bit too tight (and nothing like the plain white button-downs, no tie, in which he perpetually appeared in articles and interviews for art and culture and business magazines). I wore a pink lace miniskirt that had been designed for a shorter woman and which, when I sat, barely covered the areas that required covering—and he kept looking at me like he was in love with me, his green eyes all wide and bright and wet-looking, as he asked if I masturbated a lot, like most artists did.

"Do they?"

I didn't know many artists. At the evangelical college, those in the arts were steered toward teaching and graphic design and away from being what our department chair contemptuously and dismissively referred to as "the gallery idol."

He seemed to take my indirect answer as affirmation and then began to speak of penises in art.

"I assume you've seen *Man in Polyester Suit* by Robert Mapplethorpe?" he asked. I shook my head. He appeared incredulous. "Where was that Baptist college you went to again?" I told him, and he told me about the photograph of the black man in a suit, the frame cutting off the top of him at chest level, his sizable erection, veins exquisitely illuminated, extending out from the unzipped suit pants.

"You have to understand that white men feared the black penis," he told me, as the short, curly-haired waiter delivering our drinks glanced over at me, presumably to see how I was taking this in, and then with a professionally benign expression turned back in the direction from which he'd come. "They were concerned about its effect on women and about the danger of sexual madness that might go along with having such a large organ." He spoke of the field of comparative anatomy in the early 1800s, of scientists fascinated by the sight of African penises preserved in formaldehyde.

Speaking of formaldehyde, had I ever seen Damien Hirst's *The Physical Impossibility of Death in the Mind of Someone Living*?

I said I had read about it once in a magazine. I said I hadn't been to any museums in the UK, or New York for that matter.

"No museums? You poor thing. What are you doing here with me? You should be at a museum!" Though he sounded pleased with himself, like both of us knew better. His voice had a musical and self-delighted quality, like he was slightly above all this and amused by the fact of himself.

The gold-flecked green of his eyes glowed liquid and tender with invitation.

"They're closed," I pointed out.

"I like that—*they're closed*. Do you have any idea how you look when you say things?"

"No." It struck me as a ridiculous question, comforting in that it made him less intimidating to me in a way. "Do you?"

———

But he skipped that question to talk about me instead. "There isn't much emotion showing but there's definitely from moment to moment an expression of your level of interest. You're good at looking interested. Is it feigned? If you're good at *seeming* to be interested when you aren't and seeming to not be when you *are*, you might be good at my job." He laughed, apparently not expecting an answer. He looked like nothing I said could've surprised him anyway, like he couldn't feel surprise past a certain level (like surprise was nothing more than the feel of the wind against his bald head, ruffling nothing). "But I'm glad you're an artist. I'm so glad you're an artist and that I found you and that we're sitting here now."

He meant it. He stared at me like I was the answer to a question he'd been carrying around forever. I myself had come to New York with that kind of question; I had come especially to meet another man, H., an artist and filmmaker, whose paintings this art dealer sold. H. was the one who'd shown the dealer my work.

I wasn't sure I liked this man, though. Whatever I felt went beyond like. I wanted to like him because then whatever I felt about him would make more sense to me.

No one had talked to me like this before: in the air was the spiritual equivalent of the surface of my eyeball being almost imperceptibly palpated by one of those machines with a chin rest you stare into at the optometrist's.

I said I, too, was glad. Then we were back to penises.

"Zelda complained that Fitzgerald's penis was too small. He was said to have developed a complex about it." At this he watched me intently, as if trying to arrive at a decision. "Do you like Fitzgerald?" Before I could answer he cleared his throat, and quickly added, "Do you like literature?" as if that were the real question.

I nodded yes to Fitzgerald and to literature. "I like to read. Sometimes I write."

"What do you write about?"

"People I run into. Everyday stuff. But I guess really it's about a path to God." That was what I felt about my artwork, too, not being comfortable at church but always pursuing a belief in something, trying to close that gap between the something and me, and saying it made me brace myself in the way one sometimes does when she expects she is about to be ridiculed. But he seemed not to mind and explained to me that he, too, was religious, though an atheist, and asked my denomination; when I told him I'd recently considered becoming Catholic but didn't like their attitude toward gay people, he said he didn't think I should let that stop me from becoming one. "Really?" I said. "You don't see that as a problem?"

"Oh, it doesn't matter," he replied authoritatively.

The laughter of a woman from a few tables over distracted me. I turned to see that although older she was prettier than me. With my husband I was always aware of such women, addled by the idea of how easily he might replace me with one of them. Women liked him. Occasionally when I returned from the bathroom at a restaurant I'd come back to find him engaged more happily in conversation with the waitress than he ever was with me; with me he claimed he could be himself, which was depressed.

But if my art dealer noticed the prettier woman he didn't show it.

Then we were back to literature.

"People you run into. Like me?"

I nodded.

Again the woman's laughter rose above the general buzz of the place, teasing my ear. He smiled at it, at me; the distraction had become our amusement. There had been on his face only the briefest flicker of annoyance at my eyes darting away.

"Oh, please don't write about me," he said, as if the thought of it were already irresistible to him.

"Don't worry. It's not the kind of thing I show people," I replied.

But I wouldn't have known how to write about him then because he didn't make sense to me, everything he said seeming to have double or hidden or artfully implied meaning. But then again, possibly it didn't mean as much as I thought it did. And when I think back on the whole conversation, a lot of what we both said did and didn't make sense in a way. I mean, we regarded each other as if there were some deep and profound communication happening—he was telling me about his dead sister, about how a Christian friend had called him to check on him every day after her death to tell him he was praying for him, and though the vulnerable look of his face while saying this moved me, something about the way he said it, the way in which the wet green eyes measured my reaction, made me think he spoke of her often, to pick up women, and that this version that included the praying was the version he'd personalized for me. I didn't mind. At one time I had found my husband's pain attractive, too (abandoned by his mother, flirted with as a teenager by his stepmother, his failure to find his way as a sculptor, his frustration over his inability to "want to be happy" as he put it), but that pain in its offering had

always seemed wrung out or even flung at me; and this pain
entered the air between us as light and contained as wrapped
candy. "I read that love is what penetrates the shells we're
trapped inside," I said a few minutes later, already intoxicated,
eyeing his gesticulating hands and masculinely slender wrists,
unbuttoned sleeves sliding down as his hands moved up. Then
I was embarrassed, maybe because I was married and speaking
of love to him, or maybe just because I was speaking of love,
or because his eyes caught again my eyes on his hands. I sensed
something faintly ridiculous about both of us, like children
pretending roles (each aware of the other's true self, the de-
fining characteristic of those selves being their attraction to
each other), and when the waiter came by with fresh beer for
me, a martini for him, I experienced the rush of having been
almost found out—but found out at what?—which added to
the sense of absurdity. Around us other patrons were sitting
or rising out of chairs, having conversations and eating bread
from baskets, the summer light only beginning to dim, the can-
dles in that open-air place just beginning to be lit by the staff,
and though I'd been tired and hadn't really wanted to meet
him I was becoming distinctly aware of the sense that we and
they existed on separate planes of reality, ours being better.
Still, every time I said something it sounded odd to me, and
I was surprised that his face staring back at mine seemed to
register it as right. At that time, I should add, I was also (perpetually) afraid of saying the wrong thing and had been like
this since childhood, believing everything I said revealed too
much about me, the problem of me, to other people, the sound
of my voice converted to the sound of a pencil scratching white
expanse; but this man had expressed interest in the slides of my
pieces shown to him by H., told me they were very good—so

good in fact they verged on being bad—and admired what he viewed as the "obsession and necessity" underlying my "awkward bravado."

Three months ago the dealer and I had first spoken over the phone.

His accent had sounded refined and slightly affected. It reminded me of blazer-wearing prep-school boys in movies, as if invisibly stamped with a crest. (I disliked and was fascinated by such boys.)

"I like how you paint like you're better than you are and so in a sense become it," he had said, causing a physical twist of pain that seemed to begin with my clenched stomach and spread with an ache throughout my limbs. "I don't mean that you aren't a very good painter, of course," he said, evoking my self-disgust at the sense of balm being smoothed over a burn. I didn't want to care what he thought. But then, "You're a very good painter, obviously." So I did.

At home, on the stool in my studio I uncrossed my legs, so that the one that had been on top was now below the other. With the hand not holding the phone, I picked at my bottom lip in the childhood way I'd ceased long ago. Aware of it after the fact, I stopped. I hated and admired him for his ability to cause it.

But as we discussed individual pieces I began to feel comfortable with him, comprehending the style of his personality, and the paintings and drawings in my studio—technically the guest bedroom—in which I spent the dark insomniac hours of the morning working, began to alter before my very eyes as he violated and revered and defamiliarized them with strange eyes I couldn't see. His intrusion into my world was at least as upsetting as the week my husband's stepmother had occupied the room. ("Why are you painting all these ugly-looking men?" She'd called me up the stairs to confront me suspiciously one afternoon, having—against my request—removed the tarp I'd draped over the paintings there.)

He called me for the second time a few weeks later, and then again a week after that, seeming each time to have some specific question about my art that needed clearing up for reasons of intellectual and/or professional curiosity, each time causing me to wonder if his interest would lead to an offer of representation. But then abruptly, just when I'd lost track of time or become jarred by the awareness of it, hoping to get off the phone with him before the sound of my husband's car in the drive (the conversations about painting sounding threat-eningly intimate, his pauses, his very breath, it seemed, laced with desire), he would hang up.

The first time, I had thought some technical problem had occurred, or that he'd mistakenly hit the wrong button and would soon call back, but by now I understood that when the conversation in tension and emotion climaxed he shortly afterward ended the call.

Then, one afternoon, over the phone, around three, I finally told him that the strange men I drew and painted resembled (in one way or another) the man who had abused me as a girl. A couple of the men I'd even at first mistaken for him, I explained, stiffening and failing to breathe as I did when I encountered a potential subject in public; as I became certain of the subject not being *that man*, a predatory sensation would overtake me and propel me in the man's direction, where I would surprise and charm him into allowing me to draw and photograph him, the sittings occurring mostly at bars and coffee shops. *Excuse me, sir, I know this must sound strange and*

I'm sorry to bother you, but I'm an artist and has anyone ever told you you have the most amazing face? (Always girlishly and struck, like I didn't do this often, like I had at great personal risk come out of my comfort zone.) From these I made the paintings. Nine men had posed for me.

"I suppose you wouldn't believe me if I said I knew," he said. "I mean that I suspected something along those lines because of the, well . . . as I described to H.—who agreed with me—Schiele-like reconciliation of your attraction to . . ."—he cleared his throat—"and inherent repulsion from your subject. Your repulsion from your subject's power over you, you could say," he went on in a dreamy and intimate voice that caused me to find myself absentmindedly touching my breast and requesting, "Could you please not hang up on me this time?"

"Hang up on you?" he murmured. "I assumed you as well as I understood when our conversations ended."

(Had anyone else said this to me I'd have been stunned by his pomposity.)

Then he told me he was honored to represent me.

"You're going to represent me?" I said, staring out my studio window, at the sunny spring afternoon, a pleasurable shiver running down my spine.

"Yes," he said, amused. "I had assumed that was understood from the beginning. I don't waste my time."

At which point I pressed my hand against the window glass and wondered if having never met him I could possibly be in love with him. As I admit I wondered about H., so that I wondered if I could be in love with two men (whom I'd never met, who at times, because I'd never met them, seemed even to merge into one mysterious and powerful masculine being) in addition to my husband, who after a day of sales as a pharmaceutical representative spent most of the evening out back drinking scotch in a shed. "It's not that I don't want to talk to you," my husband explained. "It's that I have to talk to people all day and don't have anything left by the time I get done. Somebody has to make the money for you to get to stay home and paint," he said, though he'd been the one to encourage me to stay home and keep house to begin with. We were supposedly trying to have a baby, but that had gone on for a while with nothing happening and the idea of consulting a doctor embarrassed him. If I wanted *I* could visit the doctor, but he didn't plan on going. In the privacy of our home he radiated contempt for doctors because he didn't like sales (though he was good at it) and had to sell them his company's product, an antidepressant that, when he took a course of it, had absolutely no effect on him, like the others he'd tried.

Though he claimed to be working on his art in the shed, most of the time he came back inside with clean hands. He usually took his laptop into the shed with him, and I suspected he spent a lot of time drinking and watching porn.

So I felt only a little guilty about looking forward to and obsessing over the calls from the art dealer.

Sitting now before me at the restaurant he was nodding, nodding.

In my hometown my work had been dismissed by the cursory once-overs of local gallerists who seemed offended I'd have the gall to even solicit their attention, their spaces inferior to his in size and design and prestige.

And here he was, their obvious better, in the flesh, eyeing me with at least as much interest as he had given my paintings.

The restaurant we sat in was open-air and outside the partitions that enclosed it the sun was setting, the streets dimming to the blue of dusk, and I got up to accompany him as he smoked a cigarette. I hated smoking—my husband smoked—and also I was envious of the manner smokers had with each other, the way another man happened by us standing outside the restaurant and bummed a cigarette, the understanding, *the knowingness*, passing between them as smokers. As the cigarette moved to his lips, then away, his thin lips framed with beard hair, he explained to me, unnecessarily, "I have started smoking again," and I said, "Yes, I see, you're smoking," and people passed up and down the street, and we said some other things to each other that didn't matter, and again he smiled at me with that sort of private delight.

"You keep looking at my hands," he said.

At which point H., whom I'd met in person only yesterday, after having corresponded with him for a year, arrived.

———

I should say that at that time H. no longer thought of himself as a filmmaker and that his idea of himself as a failed filmmaker, to which he alluded in our correspondence, seemed evident in the way he carried himself that evening from the dark of the night toward the golden ambience of the dining area. Though he would later go on to make another experimental film for which he would receive a prestigious award, at that time he had lost his confidence and had in his posture—in his shoulders and neck—the faint but noticeable quality of a man still bracing himself from mixed reviews and financial disaster. Just before he crossed the threshold into the light of the dining area, he paused for no apparent reason and seemed to me to be hearing something from a distance (though I might have imagined this, his face cast in shadow). When he finally crossed into the dining area and neared our table, he projected the opposite air of my art dealer; the former seeming to give off the impression of not being sure he was in the right place while the latter might easily have been able to convince one of the other patrons he owned it.

As H. settled into his chair he made an expression of discomfort, began sliding the chair at an angle to the right, toward the table, but then—apparently having bumped the knees of his long legs into the table's foundation—sighed, scooted back, and somehow in the process knocked over a glass of water.

"How did you even do that?" said my art dealer, because to move his chair, H. had not needed to have his arm anywhere near the water glass. "Every time he and I go out something like this happens."

With his napkin, H. wiped the wet spot on the table, and with the one I handed him he daubed at his shirtsleeve.

As one of the waiters rushed in to help with the glass and ice on the floor, I saw H. throw our art dealer a look that he'd give him again later, that seemed to be an acceptance of the playfully bullying tone he took with H., of his delight at H.'s humiliation; and I found myself pained on H.'s behalf.

"His legs are long," I said in his defense. "The tables are a bit cramped and he's much taller than average."

"Yes," our dealer said. "But as you see, so am I."

————

I should say also that I then already had what you might call the arrogant conviction that I possess the capacity to recognize true genius, and even though H.'s silent film about the coming-of-age of a deaf and dumb adolescent boy had been criticized for being pretentious and self-indulgent, and had lost money—a noticeable percentage of audience members at a screening in L.A. had walked out during what some would refer to as pointless and tedious dream sequences—I believed (like a few of the really authentic and brave critics whose reviews I'd read when I Google-stalked H.) it to be extraordinary and misunderstood.

But I thought of him as more of a painter than a filmmaker, and it was his paintings that had a year ago, in the musty basement of a library, in an old issue of *Art Forum*, attracted my attention.

I had in fact become so taken with H.'s paintings of bats that, from a hunched-over position in a library carrel, I'd cut out the whole article, not fully admitting that I'd stolen it until out in the parking lot.

That the paintings in the article I'd stolen were of bats surprised me at least as much as my taking them, and my feelings about the bats surprised me even more. In their two-dimensional plane, the hyperrealistically painted bats hung from above, their wings wrapped around their bodies. The artist had rendered them so hauntingly (with velvety bruise-colored shadows and ephemeral blue-silver highlights) and tactilely (a pinkish flesh tone peeked out from beneath where the light hit a thin spot near the base of a bat's furry head) that for the first time in my life I fantasized about stroking one. Before, I'd been revolted by them, had in fact upon flipping through the magazine felt a flicker of that revulsion; but I'd then developed this other feeling that led me to turn back to the beginning of the article to study the photograph of the artist, a middle-aged man. While this too at first seemed unremarkable (being bald, he was not like *the man*, the abuser, from my youth, and neither slight nor classically handsome, like my

husband), upon closer inspection he transfixed me: the generous, well-meaning expression in his gray eyes coupled with a
slight but distinctive frown, as if he were simultaneously appealing to me to come closer even as he waved me away, struck
me as mysteriously and disarmingly familiar, like a face from
a dream.

Not only the skill with which the bats had been painted
but their placement within the rectangle of the canvas, and
the shape of their suspended bodies, the emotional effect of
this (the slopes of shoulders in Picasso's Blue Period paintings came to mind), lingered and even persisted long after I'd
gone back home and begun to cut vegetables for dinner. While
slicing an onion at the cutting board, I became distinctly
aware of the article in my bag, and stopped cutting to move
the bag up to my studio, after which, back downstairs, I continued to be aware of the bag as I was sometimes aware of a
painting in the midst of its creation, as if by being so at-
tached to it I myself took up two separate areas of space. It was
not a pleasant feeling but a source of constant tension; and
added to this was my now-watering, irritated eyes that I
had on the way back down the stairs rubbed with onion-tainted
fingers.

"Why are you crying?" said my husband, who'd just come in.

I said that I had gotten onion in my eyes, but at the expression of concern in his face, the softening of his own eyes in
their examination of mine, I had for reasons I couldn't understand (though in retrospect I am aware that we made rela-
tively little eye contact, that while he looked at me a lot he
much less often looked directly into my eyes, and that his
eyes searching mine like that in itself might have made me

emotional) actually begun to cry. Over dinner, I considered telling him how I'd stolen the article, considered making it into a funny story, but then the moment passed, after which I understood that I would not be telling him about it (why?); and then in the evening, after he went out to the shed to "sculpt," I again found myself drawn to the article, which I this time read on top of our made bed.

That night, when I awoke for the second time around three in the morning—the first time to see if my husband had come back in the house; he had; he was in his office with the door open, watching porn, and upon hearing me had turned toward me with that ignited, vacant expression he got, steered me back into the bedroom, fucked me (uncharacteristically, in the dark), rolled off of me and patted my thigh reassuringly before falling asleep—I knew that I would not fall back asleep, and, as a result of this feeling, got up to paint but instead found myself sitting down at the computer to type the bat artist's name into a search engine, where I discovered he had a Facebook page. Because he had not seemed to me like the type of artist to have one, I was stunned by the possibility of contact, which I hadn't until that moment considered to be possible— and after staring at the screen for what must have been ten minutes, with as much excitement as foreboding I sent him a friendship request.

———

Then for a couple of hours I worked on the painting of B., a man I'd first spotted in the street, in front of one of the best hotels in town. I had been coming from my favorite coffee shop, and as he'd come from the opposite direction and neared me we'd made eye contact. At the charge of his gaze, I'd looked away first.

With his dark eyes imprinted in my mind, I turned, headed back in the other direction, keeping a generous distance between us in case he turned around.

That day in late January, aware of the Christmas decorations having disappeared from the fronts of shops, of the absence of the wreaths that had wrapped the streetlamps, I enjoyed a sense of anticipation that eclipsed what I'd felt as a child awaiting permission to leave my room to go to the tree, and even though I was nervous I grinned and giggled so audibly that a mother holding the hand of her little son turned to smile at me. "What's she laughing about?" the kid asked. "Something in her head," the mother responded in an amused tone.

He walked with his hands in his pockets. From behind he might have been anyone—men could be like that in a way women less often were, because of their short haircuts and dark suits— and yet I already knew the back of that head and neck and shoulders well enough to, if the occasion arose, distinguish him from others of his type.

Inside the restaurant (a steak place) I spotted him at the bar and sat down two stools from him, deciding to wait to see if he talked to me first, because whenever I could afford to let them instigate contact with me, they took in the whole idea of it more comfortably.

When he first looked over I smiled absentmindedly, not like he was anyone I recognized but like he was someone to whom I meant to be mildly friendly, just because he sat near me at a bar and had happened to glance in my direction.

"Hey," he said, a moment after I'd turned away to examine the menu. "Excuse me, but did we just pass on the street, near the Westin?"

"Oh, maybe," I said, smiling and making a show of taking him in. "I was just down there. Are you staying there?"

"Yeah," he said amiably.

I was drawn to them not only for their appearance but for a certain type of loneliness about them, and they typically acted pleased by my being so open to conversation.

This time, though, things took an unusual turn when he suggested I do the drawing not at the bar but at his hotel.

"Why not here?" I wanted to know. I could not go back to his hotel room. He had the wrong idea.

"Honestly, it embarrasses me to have you drawing me in public," he said. "It's too intimate. I'm not trying to get you there to come on to you. I see your ring. I'd just rather do it in private."

Okay.

In my studio, the trance I went into when I painted was intermittently broken by an awareness of my hair and clothes smelling like smoke (my husband had quit smoking a while back but started up again, complaining that the anxiety "coming off" of me lately "drove" him to it) and a preoccupation with the memory of my husband's former smell, which I had loved but couldn't now distinctly remember, except that I had loved it. Coloring the trance itself, seemingly embedded in the strokes I applied to the canvas, was the excitement and fear of accompanying the man back to the Westin that afternoon, all the way thinking that even though he seemed like a nice enough man I should not be entering a hotel room with him alone. Inside the dim, tastefully decorated interior, I had felt relief when he immediately went over to the opposite side of the room, to the picture window there, to draw back the heavy burgundy-and-green curtains, with their dreamy under-veils of ivory muslin.

Day flooded the room. I exhaled. He turned back toward me. I found myself regarding his shoes—black, plain, well-crafted masculine dress shoes.

The sudden motion of his hand caused me to jump.

He covered his mouth as he sneezed.

"Did I scare you?" he said, entertained, relief flooding my tensed limbs. "For a second there you looked like you thought I was about to kill you."

———

Abruptly in painting I reached a stopping place—it would just come over me suddenly, that I had done all I could do at the time, that I couldn't possibly paint well beyond this point—and went back to check my email, where I found that H., who must also have painted at night or been unable to sleep, had accepted. As the sky lightened, I bled out a message to him, my emotion for his work inseparable from the words used to carry it, so that there was the sense of sending him a vessel (a message in a bottle, so to speak). The room stank of turpentine. I had cracked the window, and could hear a bird chirping in the trees behind the house.

Quietly, I treaded down the stairs, without a coat went out into the cold of the morning and stared at the filmy yolk of the sun, the words I had written repeating themselves in my head as I walked down the empty street, certain phrases snagging my consciousness, halting the flow of my thoughts, like a stuck zipper that kept me from pulling closed the neck of a jacket against the cold.

Yet I liked being stuck. I liked the letter juxtaposed with the sunrise and the blue matter-obscuring shadows of what hadn't yet been illuminated by the rising sun, and the sound of the first cars being started in drives as my neighbors prepared to leave for work.

A few days later he wrote back to me, as I both expected and didn't expect, and then I wrote back, and this went on for a year.

And so I'd come to New York to see him.

But when I mentioned my visit to the city to the art dealer, whose interest I'd by then understood to reach beyond my painting, the dealer had asked me out to dinner. Then H. had learned of it. Or in truth I told him; I told him right after the art dealer had asked me because in addition to fearing both the art dealer and H. and wishing to play each against the other (in my mind this rendered them less threatening), I wished to make H. jealous, and I believe he was because he promptly invited himself to our dinner. Immediately I reported this back to the art dealer, who seemed annoyed and suggested we meet an hour early to be alone.

———

H., with his own pale, nicely shaped bald head, was also, if you will believe it, now bearded, and noticeably older than he'd been in his photo in the magazine article.

The day before, I'd shown up at his apartment building in Brooklyn. Well, I had called first, of course; from a restaurant down the street where I sat with my friend whom I'd come to New York to visit (though truly to meet this man and his friend), I'd said, "I'm here," into the phone, after I'd had some clonazepam and wine and french fries; and he'd sounded interested in seeing me but flustered, like a bear who'd forgotten to come out of hibernation and now at two in the afternoon in August was stumbling around in his cave, trying to figure out what was happening. Alone I had walked down some streets to his place and he'd buzzed me up.

Fantasizing about this moment, I'd imagined we might be irresistibly drawn to each other.

But from the second he opened the door to take me in, it was pretty much terrifying. We didn't know each other. We had been passionately writing to each other about art, over the Internet, and had talked a few times on the phone, but I'd never even heard him cough or seen him settle into a chair.

He was no longer a voice but a man regarding me, me not only a voice but a body. I was afraid, not of him—not physically; I had the sense that he would never intentionally hurt me—but of something else obscure to me. For a moment the world seemed leached of air. I was a bee caught inside an overturned cup, throwing myself against the glass only to bounce off of it; trapped. He regarded me with mystified and anxious gray eyes behind glasses of the type my father wore. He was closer to my father's age than my own. This had been known to me technically but not felt, not real until now. Complication radiated off of him in a way that I'd up until that time been unfamiliar with. (Until then my husband's silence had possessed the most depth and texture I'd known.) I have known only a couple of men like that since. Men whose powers of observation and inner tension suffuse the air; who make me feel as if my presence is as much a problem as my potential absence.

His parents had been deaf. Scenes from his film about the deaf boy flickered vividly, hauntingly, in my memory. Though I had associated him with that deaf-mute boy—no doubt his alter ego, who he might have been, had he been born with his parents' disability—his hyperawareness suggested the opposite, a man who heard everything.

Blind bats. Deaf boy. His subjects fascinated me.

Why had I interested him?

But when for a moment, from his position on the couch, he seemed to withdraw into himself without warning, to forget me, I worried that he'd already become bored.

Because he was a genius I became apprehensive about saying things to him I hadn't had time to work out in writing, not-good-enough things, and as I sat on a low-slung sort of mini-sofa thing across from where he sat on the couch I shifted my legs in such a way that made it possible for him to see up my skirt. This skirt was black and tiered and also made for a shorter woman—then I didn't most of the time have an appetite, but was five-nine in height and had found on sale this size-zero skirt in a petite department at the mall—and while I didn't feel confident about much, I knew I had nice legs, and unable to think of anything funny or intelligent to say, my mind sludgy with the clonazepam I chewed like candy and alcohol and the dregs of crumbling fantasy, I shifted them about in hopes that he'd forgive me for not being as smart and inspired and bold as I thought I'd managed to seem in the emails. Did he like me or not? I couldn't tell. Glancing around at the photos in his living room I froze at what I understood to be a photo of H. in his late twenties, with a full head of dark hair. A cold sweat broke out above my upper lip and beneath my armpits. Outside the sky had gone overcast, it was raining, and in his living room the muted blue light of the afternoon faded into the golden penumbras of the lamps and there was a kind of tearing sensation in the air—this had been happening to me for almost a year, this kind of tearing or sometimes narrow rushing feeling in the air, as though I might've been dragged at high speed through a dark tunnel—and then H. smiled at something I'd said to him, and the feeling lifted as I became aware of myself inside the golden light.

A few moments later though, he appeared intensely frustrated. Something was wrong. (Was it my fault? Something I'd said?) He suggested we step outside for a walk.

Out on the sidewalk as we moved forward, down the unfamiliar street, past colored rows of apartment houses like the ones he lived in, he sometimes glanced over at me as he spoke and sometimes stared straight ahead, and at the corner, seeming unsure of what to do next, of what to do with me, acted as if he had suddenly been hit with the perfect idea—like in a cartoon, I could imagine a lightning bolt striking over his head—and inquired as to whether or not I might like to visit the zoo.

Sure, I said.

So we went to the zoo.

And it was there, in front of a flock of flamingos ("Do you like flamingos?" he asked me, to which I replied, "I guess. Do you?" to which he replied, "They smell horrible, don't they? I don't think about how bad this place smells when I'm alone but when someone's with me, I become aware of how much it stinks"), that I realized we were not going to fall madly in love, that it had been a fantasy and that I would go home, back to my husband, realizing whatever had possessed me had not been love but a more vague unrest that had propelled me to fixate on him, a man I barely knew, as a love object.

They are beautiful, though, H. added hopefully, of the flamingos, just before one of the males mounted the back of a female, his wings flapping hysterically as he went about having her.

Hey, the flamingos are doing it! someone said, as H. and I continued to watch them intently, avoiding looking at each other.

I had known, anyway, that he was a great artist and would only love me until someone else, someone prettier and younger, came along, at which point he'd abandon me. This man didn't have a problem attracting women. He had one, I knew, only two years older than me.

But now that I'd fallen in love with his friend, I admit I had some trouble making eye contact with him there in the restaurant.

He did prints, too. And at the restaurant as my art dealer turned his attention to his iPhone, I observed for the second time the long stained fingernail of H.'s pinkie finger, which he used to dig out flecks of fiber caught in the ink of plates. Leathery and rough with use, his hands didn't match the rest of him and by candlelight had a mittenlike appearance. When he caught me studying them, he looked down at them himself and said, "Don't go into intaglio." The flicker of a smile that followed caused me to wonder if I'd too hastily dismissed the idea of us falling for each other, and possibly, were I not already falling for my art dealer, something might have happened that night with him and me; and yet even now as I say this, I suspect that both of us were able to relax now from our muted and mysterious mutual terror of each other only because of the presence of a third party.

My dealer had apparently been scrolling through his contact list. For he was now calling women. (Though at the time I understood him to be trying to find a woman for H. so that he could be with me, later I'd discover he was calling women he'd recently slept with, hoping, I believe, like some biblical king or gangster, to assemble a table of females to which he had access.)

But the women either didn't answer or couldn't come. Outside, darkness fell around us and the men spoke to me, each vying for my attention, my art dealer occasionally trying to embarrass H. ("You called everyone constantly," he said, speaking of H.'s last breakup and throwing me a look); and fleetingly I thought of my husband, whom I worried—impossibly, confoundingly—I would never see again, the thought seeming not like a choice but like something that had already happened, him and me on opposite sides of a glass wall; and then my art dealer, who earlier, in an irritable tone, had complained to the waiter that the music was too loud, received another profuse apology from the manager, who presented him with his card and assured him that the next time he dined there it would be to his liking, and then we finished our dinners and made plans to play pool that evening in the third-floor office of the gallery over which my art dealer reigned.

There my art dealer said I was a natural. "You're a natural," he said, as I leaned forward over the expanse of green ground, sent a red numbered ball clinking into a green one, which shot down inside a hole. Though I hadn't expected a pool table inside the office of a gallery, this seemed natural, too; this pool table and lobby with a couch and individual offices behind it, the space in which my work would hang two floors below, beneath our feet. H., holding his stick, hung back, waiting his turn, and I was afraid to look at him even, or maybe especially, when I felt him looking at me. I was just aware of him, really, aware of the complexity of his presence that I knew and did not know in the way one admiring a drawing senses a way of being from the style of a line. And my art dealer, quick, jumpy really, a strange mix of restlessness and long-bodied grace, seemed to be everywhere, all eyes and hands and wrists bare in rolled-up shirtsleeves, and then after a while we finished the game—"It seems I've won," my art dealer announced, fake apologetically and pleased with himself, like a young boy who'd burped at the dinner table; "It seems you have," H. had replied irritably, giving him a long, pointed, mildly shaming look—and sat down on the couch. Or they sat on the couch, H. down at the left and my art dealer at the right, and I was posed with a choice of where to sit on the opposite couch and after a fraction of a second found myself seated directly across from my art dealer.

"Well, I just sort of let it go," H. said to him. They were talking of H.'s correspondence with a woman who had attended a retrospective of his bat paintings. Even though H. had not stopped writing to me but helped and encouraged me, I felt I was her and this had happened to me. As I'd expected—for there had been long periods of silence in which I believed H. had forgotten me, would never speak to me again, periods in which alone, thinking of him, I'd curled into a ball to cry and pray in longing and shame and fear for myself on the floor of my studio at three in the morning, being able to get back up to paint only because I saw painting, painting well, as the only thing that could place me at H.'s side—he'd stopped talking to me and never had and never would love me, and then I looked at him, really looked at him, right into his gray and beautiful and almond-shaped bespectacled eyes, and hated him, hated H. for dooming me to this never-ending longing and separation and pain; hated him for that time he'd called me from the bedroom while his current girlfriend (accompanied by her "little dog," he told me) sat in the living room waiting for him—for as I was the woman at the show I was also the girlfriend, the girlfriend waiting as H. (who had not yet put on his pants, he told me) spoke to me in a seductive whisper he would apparently never use with me in the flesh, from atop his bed, obviously getting off on talking to one woman while another unknowingly waited, with her "little dog"; and I knew that I would to punish him fuck his friend, with whom I was perhaps in love.

"I think you can just tell," the dealer was saying now, because, you guessed it, we were again speaking of that thing, of love. H. was speaking of "fixing" my art dealer up with someone he knew (someone in their social circle there in the city), but as my art dealer spoke in answer, dismissing this, saying this person H. spoke of was not someone with whom he felt in love, he was looking at me. "When you are in love, I think you just *know*," he said in a spellbound voice.

"Yes," I said, gazing back into his eyes, "I believe you do."

But that night, because of H.'s insistence that he see me back safely to my friend's apartment, I went back to stay at my friend's, the friend I'd supposedly come to the city with the main agenda of seeing. "My sister has been writing to a prisoner," she confided to me in the small, dimmed kitchen—for this was around two or so in the morning, after I'd listened to my husband's message wanting to know why I hadn't called him back, beneath the fluorescent light of her blue-and-green-tiled bathroom.

"Really?" I said, aghast. "How does she know him?"

She had been awake when I arrived. She had spoken with her sister earlier that day. They were close.

"She doesn't," my friend said. "She's never met him. She heard about him on the news and began to write to him, and then she went to visit him in jail."

"Why would she do that?" I said. "That's so crazy," I said in an amused voice, an unnecessary number of times. "So crazy," I found myself repeating as she filled me in on the rest of the story. My friend's fiancé, who was a woman, was out of town, and then because I understood she was more upset than she'd at first seemed to me in discussing it, I tried to comfort her without seeming to be coming on to her, for I'd never been in the position before of being alone at two o'clock in the morning with a woman who loved women.

Because you see I wasn't good at touching people. I mean that I was often afraid of touching people and of being touched without knowing why, except maybe for the thing that had happened to me growing up, with the man, that I'd told my art dealer about over the phone. "*The first time I thought I saw him I froze up,*" I'd told him. "*But then I saw it wasn't him. I was with a friend at a restaurant, and I had my sketchbook, and with that guy I didn't ask if I could draw him. I just started drawing him before I even knew what I was doing. It annoyed my friend that I was drawing while she talked to me.* Are you listening to me? *she kept asking.*"

But afterward, in the car, I told her who the man reminded me of and she touched my shoulder as she asked if I was okay. I knew why she'd touched me. And I knew when people needed to be touched by me, why it mattered, and I could do it but when it happened I sort of went somewhere else, even with hugs—or most especially with hugs, from anyone except my husband whom I'd known all of my adult life, whose body was like my own, from whom I couldn't get enough affection (couldn't someone please explain to me what I was supposed to be doing during this, a hug?)—but when someone I loved felt pain I could as if from a faraway place smell the need and respond, and earlier, honestly, I had not even been able to meet H.'s eyes in the cab as he'd ridden back with me, having in the street in front of the first floor of the gallery, as he'd hailed the cab, made plans with my art dealer to meet him there the next day. In the cab as H. tried to brush my lips with his I turned my head, so that his kiss got only my hair.

In the dimly lit kitchen I hugged my lesbian friend, who junior year had admitted to me that she was transferring out of the evangelical college because she was gay. (Was I a lesbian? I couldn't help but wonder, because you see up until that year, up until I began to communicate with H., I hadn't experienced the desire to touch myself or to be touched *there*, and still experienced it only when alone, when contemplating H. and his art.)

And anyway as the hug ended I informed her that I was probably in love with my art dealer, whom, at his invitation, I was going back to meet in Manhattan the next day.

"But when you got here you thought you were in love with the artist."

She made a face at me that I recognized but wasn't used to having directed at me. Then she rose to make tea. Her body bent over the stove, her face as she looked back over at me sitting at the table in the dim, lamp-lit room caused me to feel as much discomfort over the physical distance between us as I'd felt over our closeness a moment ago.

That she was beginning to worry I might be crazy bothered me less than I'd have expected.

II

But when by the light of day I stood in front of the darkened gallery window (the place closed for business on Sunday), it seemed as if I were not crazy at all but simply meeting a man I worked with for coffee, and the sense of destiny I'd felt in the taxi all the way there, as through the window I peered out at pedestrians in sunglasses and shorts, more leisurely congesting the sidewalk to wander and browse on a Saturday afternoon, had no more hold on me than a racked dress I might've noticed but not bought, had I been one of the ones to wander aimlessly about the city rather than arrive here, dreamily expecting my life to change.

Daunted by the set of buttons at the side of the door (some of their labels were missing), I worried I was pressing the wrong button, or that even if I was pressing the right one he'd changed his mind, wasn't there, and when I look back on this moment years later, the shadow of my other life, the one in which he didn't answer, or in which I didn't even press the button but instead walked away, begins.

Another mechanical sound, a click and release, answered my buzz.

And through the intercom, momentarily shrill with static, the voice I'd known long before I'd ever seen its owner: "Take the elevator to the second floor."

When, after stepping off the elevator and being buzzed through yet another set of doors, I find him standing in the gallery, he looks less than happy to see me. Except for my own footsteps against the hardwood floor and the faint hum of the air conditioner switching on, there is only silence, him acknowledging me with a curt hello and a bothered expression—like I'm interrupting him rather than responding to an invitation he himself made—then striding away from me, back to the painting he seemed to have been studying before I came in. This puts his back to me. I feel snubbed, dumbfounded. Maybe because he doesn't seem to like me anymore, or maybe just because the afternoon doesn't have the magic of the night of our meeting, he looks less appealing to me. His jean cuffs, turned up above his ankles in the style I've noticed with cosmopolite men in their twenties and thir- ties on the street, and in recent issues of the fashion maga- zines my husband subscribes to, irritate me, seeming feminine somehow.

I do like his shirt—a worn white button-down, untucked— and in the bad air of his mysterious upset with me and my fickle assessment of him, I think how stupid infatuation is, how silly I am, how we probably won't even have time to go out for coffee before I find myself back in a cab, heading toward LaGuardia.

But then:

"I'd begun to think you weren't coming."

And maybe because I hear in his tone that I've hurt him— that I *can* hurt him—everything changes.

"I'm sorry. I misestimated the travel time. I'm not used to taking cabs."

I was only fifteen minutes late, I consider, and this just for coffee on a Sunday afternoon.

Yet the feeling that I've committed the unforgivable persists. Is it my imagination?

"I may have to get away soon," he says, rather dismissively, as if some part of him were already gone. "There's something important I might have to attend to this evening."

Something in me drops. Quietly I panic. While at first my outrush of questions—about what he does, about how things work at the gallery, about my situation with him—seems practical, I realize as I'm speaking that the questions themselves don't much matter to me, that they are secondary to my reason for asking them, which is to draw him back to me. The sound of this, of my voice in the otherwise silent gallery, saturated with interest, disturbs me because I think he might be able to hear its disjointed (and desperate) relationship to the words.

But no, he believes we're really having a conversation and is in fact delighted by the questions, my naïveté. Gradually he warms to me again. We discuss the problem of value. He must create a sense of the value he sees in the paintings for other people, he explains, and the people in whom he creates this sense of value must be the right ones.

"We can't let just anyone buy them," he says of my pieces. "Do you understand how it works?"

There on the second floor, he stands in front of large-scale oil paintings of what appear to be lower-class Southerners engaged in domestic dramas. In one of them a woman clutches a yowling infant to her chest while a man in jeans and a soiled white undershirt yells at her, his hands thrown out, his face taut with fury and pain. And in another, a woman in cutoffs and a tank top holds a pool stick javelin-style, at the threshold of a bedroom, pointed at a nude woman with a deer-caught-in-headlights expression standing in front of a bed where a man (whom they both obviously desire) sits also nude, the navy sheet cast over one luminously rendered bare leg only partially obscuring his groin.

That painting is in fact titled *Deer Caught in Headlights*, and I suspect he directed me here, to this floor, to see it.

"But what do you mean?" I want to know. "Don't you have to let whoever offers the price have them?" I say.

"No. Of course not. It's good I got ahold of you before you started throwing it away. The wrong collectors would devalue your work."

"But it seems unfair to be so exclusive about it," I argue, for by the light of his returning attraction to me—palpable in the way his eyes cling to my movements, follow my hand reaching down to adjust the strap of the flimsy sandals I'm wearing that day—I've begun to feel the beginnings of obstinacy, of the casual resistance a woman can assume around the man to whom she by instinct already knows herself bound.

"Ah, but it'd be unfair the other way too, wouldn't it?" he replies. "Do you think some dumb trader yuppie is going to understand what you're doing? That there's no difference between someone like that and L [a name I don't recognize] having your work? Knowing how to display it? To whom to lend it? By what context to interpret its necessity?"

You need me, is what he seems to be saying. And, *I saved you*. I read between the words. In his green eyes. In the pregnant pause in which I feel his continuing awareness of the painting behind him, the painting he wishes for me to admire.

"It's by a Swiss painter," he tells me. "He has never been to the South but is obsessed with American country music videos.

This is what he imagines the American South to be like. These are his fantasies. Aren't they fascinating?"

Nodding, I think I might hate them but am fascinated by his fascination, by how he sees. I say something about the use of color in them, and in a manner I'd identify as pretentious, had someone else been talking, go on about the biblical implications of the use of purple throughout. The knowledge that I need to pull my phone from my purse to check the time distracts me; I sense if I do this he'll take even that brief loss of attention as a slight, so I go for the direct approach, bring up that it's almost time for my flight; and what about those contracts he mentioned when asking me to meet him, the paperwork I could sign here instead of receiving through the mail?

"Ah, contracts," he says, eyes sweeping to take in my ringed left hand. "I use them because it makes everyone feel better, but personally I think they're silly. Don't you?"

Realizing I am not going to answer, he begins to describe the hanging system, and as he does this he reaches for me, his hand lightly encircling my wrist to draw me closer, where he then positions me between his chest and the painting affixed to the wall.

His hands at either side of my bare upper arms, he directs my focus straight ahead, toward the middle of the work. The rush this gives me causes a backlash of helplessness; I try to will myself into feeling nothing, worried he'll know.

The work is such-and-such dimensions, which is x number of inches from the floor, meaning the center of the work is at x inches, and that sort of thing—all very specific and logical but nothing more than nonsense being murmured into my hair, into my ear, in comparison with the explicit thrill of his touch and breath; of the laundered scent rising from the shirt he must have owned for years, must have worn thin and soft with the heat and exertion of his upper body and put on again and again.

"Before, this one was there and that one was here," he explains. "But I called my assistant to come in and help me switch them. I told him they were in the wrong order. He put them like this because he thinks the one with the baby belongs after the one with sex. But this one is better, so I think it should be viewed *after* the other one. Because of its excellent handling of jealousy. I am a very jealous person. It radiates off this one, doesn't it?" He pauses, seems to be considering whether or not he should say what he's thinking. "My assistant is very good-looking. Everyone notices. I rushed him out of here before you came in because I didn't want you to see him."

That he's made this confession seems to surprise him as much as me.

"He was irritated with me," says my art dealer. "I think he was with his girlfriend when I called him to come in earlier." He makes a face suggesting the whole idea of this, of his assistant having a girlfriend, is humorous to him. "They hate when I call them in on the weekends we're closed, but they've come to expect it because they know it's when I most like to work. Usually I'd be working now," he says. "And I suppose I am," he observes, it seeming to have only just now dawned on him that his switching the paintings had coincided with *this*. With us.

"But I suppose you wouldn't be, would you? Because you work late at night," he added, surprising me by remembering it. "I suppose at home around this time you'd be about to make dinner for your husband, yes?"

This last part is put to me in a falsely light tone, undercut with accusation, but is quickly followed by his saying how sad he is to see me leave.

"I am too," I reply.

"Yes, it's too bad you have to go now. I feel like we could've talked for hours and hours."

"Yes," I agree. "Me too."

When in front of the yellow cab he's hailed for me, he—burdened with my luggage, having only just set down on the sidewalk my suitcase that he instead of wheeling (as I would've) carried, my backpack still flung over his shoulder—asks me to spend another night in town with him, to let him pay for another flight home the next day, I have the sensation of this all having happened before; of my existing in a reality in which I've already even before I answer said yes; and so at the same time I make a choice there is the other feeling—that there isn't one.

Yet, even then, as the annoyed driver pulls away and we head back in the opposite direction from which we've come, I tell myself I am not going to fuck him but am staying over just to talk with him, to get to know him, and that if we do not stay up talking through the night we will certainly sleep apart.

The late afternoon is humid. Damp patches of shirt cling to my back. The prematurely darkening sky insinuates a storm that except for the briefest, lightest spray of drops that will fall later before dinner—so insignificant as to cause us to disagree over their existence (*it's raining; no, it's not*)—will never come.

Walking beside him I'm reminded of a girl following a boy who's asked her to dance, and he, peacock-style, suspecting but not certain I'll sleep with him, tells little stories of famous and wealthy people I've read about only in magazines, hoping to further impress me. "He had a tantrum with Henry once, screamed at him," he tells me of a famous artist who is known for his meek and childlike manner. "He acts guileless to keep people from being turned off by how monstrously arrogant he is. But he's a very good host. He likes taking in abandoned dogs. He has one of the ugliest dogs I have ever seen—the thing was a burn victim—and dotes on it, kisses it on the *mouth*, in front of everyone who comes over, and I've never been able to figure out if it's genuine or part of his act." Despite the criticism, the dealer's voice glows with something close to reverence. "Though to suggest they're distinguishable even to him is maybe just wishful thinking on my part."

"It's too bad you didn't get to see the twin towers," he says, though we aren't near where they'd have been, his remembering them seeming to be provoked by an actual set of attractive twin girls strolling past in polka-dot sundresses. "That was what I always looked forward to seeing the most when we visited as a kid. I like repetition," he says pointedly, as if this has something to do with me. "Damien Hirst called the attack 'visually stunning.' He said they achieved what no one would've ever thought possible. That it changed our visual language. An airplane became a weapon. People started panicking when they saw one close to a building." As we walk, he alternates between staring ahead and turning down toward me to observe my reactions. "He said, 'On one level they kind of need congratulating.'"

And what to make of this? The cold detached gaze of the art world strikes me as terrifying. But I know he means to shock me.

What is it about a man carrying your luggage, the way it appears lighter in his grip? The way you feel both grateful and entitled, in that if he hadn't offered to carry it he wouldn't be a gentleman, would be disrespecting you as a woman? Because he desires me I enjoy the display of his strength, and the memory of his rolled-up sleeves in the gallery, of the physical labor of him and the assistant having moved the large canvases before I came in. I like thinking of him holding a hammer—something about him equal parts dandy and brute. I like thinking of his gallery. Of his ability to have established it. Of his expertise. I like to think about what he does all day, from the moment he climbs out of his bed; sees his bearded face in the mirror; slips on his socks. I like the way he walks and speaks and his boyish bravado, the air of performance about him, or rather, the chinks in which I glimpse that I'm being given a performance by a very shy younger man who himself wouldn't even speak to me without the assistance of this other man who now runs the show.

But when after our first comfortable spell of silence he says, "Why *did* you like the bats so much? Those paintings?" I recall for whom I came and to whom I belong—him third on the list in terms of the men in my life—and the hint of conquest in his voice lets me know that all this time he's kept in mind what I'd forgotten.

———

"I have a sentimental attachment to this apartment," he says before leading me into the main building, adding that he prefers small spaces. Then, "This was where I moved after my sister died." While he speaks, he holds open the door for a young woman in running clothes, exiting from the other side to pass through, and says, "Hello, there. Having a jog?" and though the girl looks at him like she thinks he's a weirdo, the hint of a question at the end of her *Yeah*, the way her eyes slide over to appraise me, continues to bother me even after we're up the stairs, inside the apartment.

The faint scent of cat and incense presents itself to me as we stand inside the apartment. (We've stopped by on our way back to the gallery, from which he needs to email a file saved on his computer.) Its perimeters only a little larger than a walk-in closet, the place is about the size of my husband's former college dorm room, and now I understand why on our way here he seemed to have been trying to explain it (or even apologize for it) to me.

He has let me in to take a shower. "The bathroom," he says, gesturing toward it with his hand. Then he steps inside it, comes back out with a towel he extends to me.

"The puss is shy. She may or may not make an appearance."

His eyes spark. It takes me a second to understand he's talking about his cat. I can imagine him bursting into laughter or even dance, such is his giddiness at having me inside this space; after he shuts the door to go wait at a bar next door, I can't decide if he likes me more than my husband ever did or if what he feels rides more on the surface of him than it does with most; if he likes me in an exceptional way or (again worrying over his reaction to the jogger) if he just likes women. *She'll sleep with him after I'm gone*, I think, remembering how her eyes went over me and then back to him. *It doesn't matter; you're married.*

The door to the bathroom doesn't shut all the way, and in the shower I find nothing to wash with but an amber bar of honey-scented soap.

Outside the shower, drying myself, standing outside the bathroom so as to escape the steam, I observe a big discount jug of scotch (my husband's brand, I discover with an ache of guilt so briefly debilitating I feel almost as if it's coming from some outside force) on the narrow counter of the sink that seems to double as the "kitchen."

As I sit on the edge of his single bed, I text my husband to tell him both that my flight has been changed to the next day, and that I seem to be having problems with my cell phone; but as I type I'm alarmed by a loss of sensation in my hand— like I'm staring at something that isn't a part of my body anymore—and again there's that rushing of air, as if in a tunnel, the sense of something tearing and darkening, so that I have to pull my legs onto the bed and lie down until it stops. The orange cat that has apparently been hiding beneath the bed leaps on top of it to observe me. Meowing, rubbing up against me, she seems to be begging for my affection, but after only a moment of petting (during which her soft body purrs) she rears her head back and bites my hand—hard, so hard that I cry out as she leaps down and back underneath the frame.

III

Back in the office he couldn't stay on the couch with me for more than a couple minutes; he was restless; he stood. He walked over to the window through which the now-golden last part of the afternoon lit the glass, and he told me how he hadn't had a girlfriend until after college, at the age of twenty-two. "I couldn't even talk to women," he said, lighting a cigarette. He smiled. It was as if he were talking about someone else, and again I had the sense of two men, each of them wanting to impress me with his contrast to the other.

"I worked in the library in college," he said. "I was obsessed with this woman who came in almost every day. A graduate student. She looked like a young Isabelle Huppert. Some of her blouses looked like negligees. What do you call them?"

"Camisoles," I said, pleased to know something he didn't.

"Camisoles. She'd wear these camisoles under blazers. White. Pink. Champagne. No bra. Remarkably poised. Some inborn nobility about her. Small-breasted but large-nippled. I could see them occasionally when she was leaned over her books, these rose half-dollar-size areolas. Forgive me if I'm going into too much detail, I—"

He would plan things to say to her. He'd write them down and then practice saying them in a way that sounded casual, but whenever he saw her he froze up, couldn't say anything at all, and if she came toward the desk when he was behind it, he acted busy with something else so the other clerk would have to help her.

"Finally, one day at a bar near campus, she approached the booth I sat in. She looked at me like she recognized me; she smiled; it was like being in a dream. I could tell she was about to ask me something. She appeared hopeful. She was wearing one of the champagne-colored camisoles I'd dreamed about her in. This was the closest I'd ever been to her. She was wearing perfume—very light and clean, not what I'd have imagined she'd wear but strong enough to momentarily override the smell of my food, the bar. She leaned in toward me."

At this he brought the cigarette to his lips, inhaled. Held my eyes. "She said to me, 'Are you using that ketchup?'"

"A decade later I ran into her at a party. She looked pretty much the same except that her face was leaner. She had remarkable bone structure, I saw. I could see she was going to age well. She wore a man's gambler hat. It looked perfectly ridiculous. Upsettingly sexy. She felt she knew me but didn't know from where. I didn't tell her. I pretended not to know. She was . . . *receptive*." This said pointedly, him staring into my eyes. "But she turned out to be boring and not very intelligent."

This twist in the story caught me off guard. The air changed. I felt a little like I was being warned.

"So you went out with her?" I asked.

"Out with her? No. I could tell from that short conversation at the party she was terribly dull. I had to make an excuse to get away from her. It was such a disappointment for me— here I was with the woman of my dreams on a summer night, but just *not* into it, just wanting to get away; what she was saying didn't even make much sense to me; I couldn't decide whether or not I even liked her voice, really—and at the same time, as the girlfriend that I almost married pointed out once, what I was in love with was her image, and I'd had it that year in the library. All that time I'd thought I was missing out on something, on *more*, but what interested me was there all along. I still remember her outfits. I remember how her hair looked when she came in from the rain. One day she wore this awful yellow shirt and I felt less attracted, like I'd made a mistake. The next day when she looked right to me again I felt like we'd made up. Now that I've been in some relationships, I understand that they're not much more than that, essentially, but involve talking and sex."

He exhaled. The smoke from his cigarette was a blue haze. The window overlooked the gray wall of the building across the street, speckled russet in places with discoloration. In retrospect I would think a relationship is nothing like staring at a woman in a library who doesn't know you're watching her for a year—and what I think now is that when he finally did have the chance to be with her, he just chickened out, wanting it to end with his feeling superior—but there in his office what he'd said sounded profound to me and more than likely this had to do with the way his pants fit his ass, and his way of bringing the cigarette to his lips, his knobby carpal bones giving way to long tapered forearms; the almost prissy quality of his perpetually critical air riding over some raw and puritanical desperation about this world that would never be good enough for him; and I don't know how to explain it, but there was something thuggish about him around the edges; something a little seedy not concealed by fine brands of clothes; I could imagine him in jail. Was I being typical?

"But you could say my first love was my sister," he said, going on about other women. "At the age of five I believed we'd marry, like our parents, and when I told her about it she called me an idiot and explained brothers and sisters couldn't do that. I was devastated. She was the center of my existence. She regularly broke my heart, and had we not been related she'd have had nothing to do with me. I asked her this before she died, and she confirmed it, happily. She said, 'Of course not. You're such a creep.'" His face was pleased as he said this—he loved his sister's sense of humor, I could tell, and I liked it too, and maybe this was when I began to like him. "She was so . . . she was . . ."

Then he stopped. As if shaking himself from nodding off into a dream. He was staring at me again.

"You look hungry. It's time to eat."

But at the restaurant I grew detached as I sat at the table alone while he lingered up at the front, flirting with a waitress he knew. The waiter taking my drink order noticed, too, seemed to pity me, and as I sat there in the air-conditioned dining area wearing his jacket over my tank top, I regarded him with the safe humor of a married woman on an outing with a cad: a cad whom once, now to her own amusement, she'd actually imagined herself to be in love with despite that he was so obviously—

Did I tell you, as we ate, I decided you were the saddest man I'd ever known? Loneliness clung to you. "Her fiancé is Albanian," you said of the waitress after you'd finally sat down to join me. "She's Italian but he's Albanian, and he speaks her language but she doesn't speak his. They see an English tutor together." You seemed to like thinking this at the same time you gave off a hint of jealousy. "I come here on Tuesdays, usually." In the brief lulls in conversation, when your face fell, I could see: you were one of those miserable bachelors who went to the same restaurant on the same day each week and had fantasy relationships with your waitresses. You spoke of the details of her life as one inside something, as one having entered a much larger construction, so that I pictured you with your head against a pillow, dreaming of sitting beside her as she saw the tutor, your Tuesday waitress with the olive complexion and cascade of dark curls and full chest, dreaming of stealing her from her fiancé like—

But now you were with me. Recalling your face in front of the cab, I saw now and then the glow of triumph, of the fantasy of me having become reality, the sense of increased possibility with which you viewed the waitress just before your attention turned to me. If it could happen with me, then why not with her?

And frankly by then I'd decided to sleep with you as an act of compassion. Poor thing—that night, I'd never seen anyone who so needed to be fucked. You were the kind of sad person who'd become so numb he didn't even know what sadness was anymore, who thought he was fine because he couldn't even remember being happy, and I wanted to help you.

Happy. I saw I was making you happy. I had forgotten what it was like to make someone happy.

"They were fucking," I told you. "First it looked like they were about to get into a fight—they were snapping their beaks at each other, the female snapped up at him and the male snapped down. They kept snapping like that, like they were threatening each other. But then it seemed to be more like a dance. Like an imitation of a fight.

"Then he was on her," I said. I was describing the flamingos from my trip to the zoo with H. "He climbed on top of her." I loved your widened eyes, the air of victory that came over you at just the mention of him because I was here with you now.

"He was flapping away while he stood on top of her—it looked kind of like he was trying to kill her. *What's happening?* some little kid was shrieking at his mother.

Hey, the flamingos are doing it, said someone else.

"Then H. turned and looked down at him. He said, 'The flamingos are mating. That is the male mounting the female.' 'What's mating?' the kid said back. The mother gave H. the most irritated look, and then she dragged the kid away. Oh, you should have seen it," I said. "The kid kept turning back to look at H. He looked like he wanted to get back to H. so he could find out what was going on. H. sounded so grim and serious but the kid wasn't at all afraid of him. He was like this huge man, grimly towering over the kid, but the kid looked crazy about him."

"If only he had got that reaction from you," you said dryly, both ruffled by the mention of him and pleased with yourself, before launching into your disappointment with a piece in his last series, a piece which, had he applied your advice, would have been so much better.

"I was a little embarrassed by it," you admitted. "That I got the price for it I did had more to do with my having dared to *ask* that price than the quality of the piece."

And with a rush of ardor and loyalty and guilt—with an inner flinch, as if you'd with your words struck me—I praised H.'s brilliance, his superiority as an artist, the superiority of his way with form, his vision, his originality, his depth. To you who represented him. To you who spoke of him with a faint trace of possession and condescension, as if it were the other way around.

"I am crazy about him," I said. "Just not in the way I expected to be."

"Oh," you said, smiling. "And in what way is that?"

IV

But what most affected the painter in the late-night conversation with the gallerist on the couch in the lobby that preceded their lovemaking that she even then tried to convince herself might not (and probably wouldn't) happen—this accompanied by candlelight, the backdrop of the city framed by the perimeters of the glass wall, a record player at low volume emitting *Blonde on Blonde*—was his speaking of his sister, who'd gotten cancer after he'd convinced her to move here to the city to work and who because she didn't like their stepmother didn't want to go back home to Tacoma—their real mother was gone, she'd long ago left their father for another man, and as an adult the gallerist had completely cut her off, refusing even to answer her letters, speaking to her only through his sister—and she moved in with him to die.

Then he was twenty-two, a bartender and adjunct instructor in art history at a community college in Queens.

Small. Petite. Her eyes as dark as his fair (the painter would later learn from pictures). A former librarian.

"Not the mousy kind," he clarified. "The kind everyone gets a crush on."

And on the couch in the office of his gallery he'd told the painter about how once his sister (the only one he trusted through the divorce, maybe the only one he ever trusted) after she'd given up on the chemotherapy had gotten mad at him for some innocuous comment that she'd taken in her fever as a direct attack at the heart of her being—"You use too many paper towels," he'd said, tired and only half even paying attention, but she'd heard something entirely different.

"Well you were the one who insisted," she said to him. "You insisted," she rasped at him, trying but failing to yell. (Her skin appeared scaly in places. Almost as if picked at. The odd white flecks of skin caught in the light like the pills on a thinning, overwashed sweater.) And then fifteen minutes later on the

couch—which smelled of death and cat urine and Lysol—
he'd rubbed her feet to calm her down; gotten up to go to the
bathroom; and then come out to find her gone. Terrified,
he'd hurried out of the apartment afterward but really there
had been nothing to worry about because she was just down
there in the lobby at the foot of the stairs, sitting and already
out of breath.

"Sometimes when the health-care worker didn't come, I had
to bathe her," he said, at this point the painter's persistent sense
of her art dealer's desire to kiss her having dissipated. *No, he is
not going to make a move*, she thought. Nothing was going to
happen. (Was she relieved or disappointed?)

"But it wasn't like you'd think it would be," he went on,
oblivious that he'd withdrawn himself from her as he entered
the past. "It wasn't such a big deal. Once I got started, it all
became rather abstract."

Then to her satisfaction returning to her, rearranging himself
in his seat, leaning forward: "I have some pot in my desk
drawer we could have but when I smoke it I become amorous.
I might make an advance." He smiled at her. He seemed happy
to look at her.

"So I think I probably shouldn't get it." He watched her
face. "That is, unless you don't mind."

———

The boy who when she was eight surprised her by after asking if
he could see her hand, kissing the back of it before dropping
it, running away; the boy she made out with at a movie theater
in eighth grade who the next week made out with her best
friend; the college-dropout construction worker she stayed
with on weekends as a junior in high school who lived above

an old woman's garage in what they call a "butler's apartment"
who spent a lot of time going down on her with various tech-
niques he'd read about in books, none of which made her feel
anything but that she should feel *something* that he wanted
to keep practicing despite this anyway; other young men who
touched her, bought her food, said she was pretty; the one in
college who after having on-and-off sculpted her for a year—
she has made an impression on him and so now he makes an
impression of her in the clay that will when he is done make
her cry because it looks exactly like her (it is for some reason,
she knows, so hard to make what you see; why?)—claimed he'd
done it because he'd known he'd ask her to marry him all
along; the way she learned to recognize him from across campus when he was barely recognizable except for his gait and
the vague dark slash of his form; waking up with this man, the
sound of him turning the water on and off and on again when
he is getting ready in the morning in the bathroom as she
stirs; the rumble of his car engine in the drive that she'd wait
for every evening; the patter of his footsteps climbing up the
stairs to the porch, the surge of happiness in her body stirred
by the click of his key in the lock, the swoosh of the opening
door; *he is home*, finally; the way at night she watches him in
his sleep loving him more than she could stand when he was
awake, thinking she will have to kill herself if he dies; the way
her entire being feels suddenly fragile when he in a new suit of
which he is proud steps out into the world; the way when she is
not expecting it he reaches out to stroke her hair, her neck,
*I still love you, I still want you, I haven't forgotten who you are even
though it seems that way sometimes*, but all of this in her twenty-
eighth year obliterated by the problem of the first man, by the
sense of incongruity in the darkened childhood bedroom, so

that all the others seem nothing more than versions of the same thing that she can't get back inside of as experiences of significance, that seem to be missing something important she can't understand, that run: *Once a boy I liked liked me back and he bought me food, maybe we danced, we touched, each of us said the other was good-looking and that we liked to see each other and we confessed and promised things to each other and—*

"That he couldn't see me was part of it, I guess," she told her art dealer of the artist she'd written to, his friend H., whom she'd come to the city to meet, with whom she was and was not in love. "It turned me on that we couldn't see each other."

Though she wasn't used to being "turned on," she said it not like it was a mysterious and (to her) fantastical thing that had upended her world as she knew it by occurring, causing her to feel compelled to touch herself like other people did: *How strange to want to touch yourself like you are more than yourself, to become the object of yourself that you by touching can give pleasure to; oh that is what they mean; it makes sense now; pleasuring yourself,* she thought in bed with a book showing good prints of his paintings, gotten through interlibrary loan from a college, for which she'd had to wait a month, as she stared into the paintings, feeling down there, attempting to block out the self-consciousness of her hand being down there.

Turned on by the paintings made with his hands. His voice. His hands. What his eyes that could not see her typing in front of a computer screen in another state saw.

They couldn't see each other. He couldn't see her. They could see a few photos of each other, but she couldn't feel him seeing her, this man whose vision compelled her. There was no sense of being watched by a man as the gallerist in that moment watched her, as if he could with his eyeballs stroke even her innards; his eyes; the pressure of his gaze; the narrowed feeling in the air; his eyes.

Yeah, it turned me on.

In that dumb way other people said it. Dumb in that people feeling lust had up until then seemed to her like drunken people, drunk on something that was to her unavailable.

"Writing H. was like the sky blowing open," she told him. "Everything looked different, even. The whole world seemed to have a pulse that I could feel through anything. It was like I was connected to everything somehow."

"Yes, it sounds like you got quite carried away," he replied, leaning forward to refill her glass.

———

The sexiest man she'd ever seen. On a bicycle. Something about the way he held his shoulders, his profile, his posture atop the bike, the shape of his bald head—she wasn't accustomed to seeing grown men on their way to social engagements riding bicycles, how odd, sweet; is it him or is this just how it is in the city?

"That's him. That's the art dealer," she said to her friend whom she'd begged to wait with her at the restaurant. He looked like the photos from the Internet but also not like them; much better somehow. "It's okay for you to leave now. Go on and leave, okay?"

———

And at home in a bungalow in Georgia she shared with the man to whom she was married, the painter in the guest room/ studio studied photos on the Internet of the famous artist with whom she corresponded, her paint-stained hands typing into the keyboard intermittently a curious sight to her, as if the hands of someone else. (Should she paint these hands? This for the first time considered.) A tall bald man with a beard he wore a dark suit among other sophisticated-looking people in fine clothes, and this was from seven years ago—but how did he look right now? she wondered—and mostly partially blocking the figure of another famous artist she recognized was another tall, bald man with a beard, a good deal younger, who to her was no one of name or consequence but simply the body of a man dressed nondescriptly, whom she'd never have noticed had he not been blocking the visage of the famous artist, who didn't really seem to belong there but was nevertheless there in the way.

————

Meek and shy and very quiet but there was a tendency toward destruction of personal artifacts—words she'd written on paper and pictures she'd painstakingly painted and twice her hair that she'd with her mother's sewing scissors lopped off into the sink. Taking a baseball bat to the piano is only a silly fantasy but when no one else is in the house if you bang very hard against the keys until your hand aches it falls out of tune and all the notes that would usually when played together make a song bleed a strange half melody that—

No, not sad. Quite perversely happy when the only photo in the living room in which she as a girl posed alone fell into the toilet and she for her mother had to create the most absurdly plausible story to provide an explanation for how the photo had come to be needed to be taken into the bathroom and then by accident become drowned in the water.

————

And then a pale pink sliver of trout fell from her fork into her lap. The skirt onto which it fell was on this night sporty and cheap, soft and gray, as was his plain button-down shirt (all of the buttons except the top closed this time, the shirt a dove-gray, a much paler gray than her skirt, causing him to rather look more like the adjunct art history instructor he'd once been than the glamorous character she'd followed around all afternoon).

And when she moved the sliver of meat from her lap to the surface of the table he, watching, always watching, picked it up and put it in his mouth, and she was happy in a way she hadn't known before.

———————

Her first—the first man—would say his head hurt, would she please turn out the light because it was hurting his eyes which was causing his head to ache?

Already he would've reclined onto the bed from which he'd cleared the extra pillows and stuffed animals, exposing the bare flat surface of the bed that when she was alone frightened her, so that she'd crowd the animals with whom she conversed when alone around on either side. He was a very big man the tallest she knew with thick dark hair his thighs nearly as thick around as her girl waist. In college he played on the basketball team and when others were around and he wished to interact with her he'd style her hair. A movie-star hairstyle he called it, brushing her long hair from around her shoulders, from off her back, and pulling it into a ponytail that was pretty much like the one her mother made yet in his hands didn't seem to be the same hairstyle at all but truly the hairstyle of a celebrity, which is better than the hairstyle of a normal person—

You know (stereotypically, as this sort of thing often goes): in addition to being a family friend, the babysitter.

The wet, she believed, the unmentionable embarrassment of a grown-up having let his bladder go.

Mainly just a sense of incongruity. The feeling that something beyond her understanding that was strange and uncomfortable but that pleased the man who was her admirer had occurred and in truth she was happy to be with him because he seemed to like to be alone with her more than anyone else she had up until that point in time known.

———

"Have you done this before?" says the man in the hotel room. Before she can speak, taking his answer from her face, he says, "How many times?"

Not knowing whether he will find the number too high (making this seem less significant) or too low (causing her to seem inexperienced), she replies, "This is the first time I've done it in a hotel room like this."

"I hope it's the last," he says. "You shouldn't have followed me in here alone."

His concerned and curious face is something like paternal.

He watches her like he doesn't trust her, like she might be up to something more than drawing, but he can't figure out what it is.

"Are you going to let me draw you, or did you just invite me in here to admonish me for not being afraid of you?"

On the couch she shifts her legs, opens the sketchbook to a clean page. From the pouch in her purse in which she keeps her drawing utensils she extracts a special graphite stick her husband ordered from a French website and presented to her Christmas morning.

That he would be angry and alarmed about her being here occurs to her, but it also seems of only mild significance, like a scene in a movie that pulls at the emotions but has nothing to do with real life.

"But you *are* afraid of me," he replies incredulously.

She has begun to draw. She doesn't answer.

Am I? she thinks. And, as she studies his face studying hers, *How do I look to him?* She wears one of her better outfits (tall black leather boots with silver buckles, a wool skirt, a snug white cashmere sweater with a low V-neck, and beneath that a white lace push-up bra). She has put on makeup.

With graphite she blocks in the dimensions of his face.

"Did you follow me to that restaurant?"

"Do you hope I followed you?"

This comes out more flirtatiously than she means for it to, as it has on other occasions over the past few years; with her husband's boss, for example, at a buffet table at a Christmas party, soon after which the man "accidentally" brushed up against her, infuriating her husband, who could not until they were safely out of earshot of any of the other employees, in the car, vent his rage. *Do you want to fuck him?* he snapped, his eyes hateful, vigilant for any reaction from her he might use as confirmation. She ignored him, stayed quiet, still. As he drove he described under his breath the things he believed she wanted to do with his boss that if she'd confronted him about he'd deny having said. This had happened before—him saying things he later denied. It made her feel crazy. An hour later, at home, the anger turned to lust (the lust, as she understood it, having as much to do with his boss as her), and afterward her husband seemed to love her again; it was just a bad night.

"No," she tells the man she is drawing, before he can answer the question she posed in return, in case he attempts to flirt back with her. "No, I didn't follow you. I just recognized you at the bar and thought, *This is the second time I've seen him now, so I just have to draw him.* Your face stayed with me. You have that kind of face."

This devoid of flirtatiousness. Said clinically. Authoritatively.

He seems to accept it.

The fantasies of what they might do instead—of him reaching out to place his hand on her knee, of him rising up in the middle of the sketch to push away the sketchpad and put his mouth on hers—flash intermittently as if on a movie screen at her periphery, a movie she isn't watching but doesn't have the power to turn off. Sometimes she doesn't know the men are handsome until afterward, studying the sketches that, though not flattering, accurately show the structure of the faces, the eyes.

"I want to see it," he says after.

And it is this moment she both anticipates and fears; she can't very well *not* show it to him.

The book in his hands makes her anxious because she imagines him ripping out the pages, tearing them up, even though this has never happened with a sketch she's shown to anyone.

He stares at her as if seeing her now for the first time. Looks back at the sketch. His fingers go up toward his temple, hover there without quite touching it before curling, pressing briefly against his mouth. He looks back up at her.

"I don't know whether I should be flattered or offended."

Both, she thinks. But she says nothing. Waits.

"Let me take you out to dinner."

"You just ate dinner."

"I know," he says, flustered, amused. "I mean—"

"I'm married," she replies.

But by then I had changed my mind. We were so drunk.

Or I was, at least (the beer before dinner and then the bottle of wine during it and in the office of the gallery the cognac that had been given to him by a collector that I continued to drink even with the feeling of it being impossible to take in any more because my voice talking sounded better to me when intoxicated), and I'd started to lose the light and the light coming off him was fading too; and when he asked if I wanted to smoke the pot that would make him amorous, I said that was fine, it didn't matter I was married anymore as nothing seemed to matter there high up above the city in the dark; and now all the lights were off in the office too, us being able to see by the security lights shining out from the windows of rooms of the building opposite and from streetlights below and from the front part of the office in front of the wall that was almost all glass; and we moved toward the other way into the darker area behind us, toward his personal office space where he'd told me the story about the woman from the library who'd disappointed him with her dullness and lack of intelligence; and fortunately there, there was another big window through which emitted faint light that kept the office from being entirely black inside and by this faint light I was enraptured by the sight of the fingers of his long graceful hands nimbly unbuttoning his shirt—

Oh, wait, I forgot to say we smoked the pot. By now he had rolled the joint and we'd passed it back and forth and had become high.

My first time since high school.

I coughed. Briefly I struggled. (How unattractive did I become coughing? At least it was dim.) But then it worked: I was high.

More talking. Not the kind that matters. Just something to do until he works up the nerve to kiss me, and then—

I want you. Baby, I want you. I want you so—

A firm, deep kiss; no playing around before he shoves in his tongue.

This goes on for a minute before he abruptly pulls away, saying he needs to roll another joint.

"I think the music is playing again."

"Is it? I think it might be you."

"I'm surprised you keep that in here," I go on, not wanting the silence.

"Oh, it's not a big deal," he says, just as casually. It's more like the kiss has interrupted our conversation than the other way around. He stands bent over his desk but it's too dark for me to see his expression. "We call and someone brings it here." But then after the fact, the addendum, voice more pointed and emboldened: "I'm a risk-taker. I don't think you're really doing your job unless you're constantly risking the loss of it," he said, I comprehending he was no longer talking about the pot.

While he's rolling the joint, watching his hands, I begin to undress.

He turns.

Oh.

Facing me, he lights the joint, inhales.

He passes it to me; after I've taken another hit, he takes one; and then after I've taken my second he, crouching down so that he's level to me on the couch, again presses his mouth against mine, hungrily shoves in his tongue.

"You too," I say, my fingers at the buttons of his shirt. "Take your clothes off."

"Not yet," he whispers, brushes my hands away.

Then we're standing, him leaning down to me for another
kiss, even more forceful, as he shoves his hand up my—

Jab

Jab

Jab

*The fingers not forming an actual fist but held straight and as
close together as possible, beaklike, forming what is also referred to
as "the silent duck."*

Briskly, matter-of-factly, with also each time a jerk.

(*Warning: can cause laceration or perforation of the vagina, result-
ing in serious injury and even death; also sexual activities that cause
air to enter the vagina can lead to a fatal air embolism.*)

But at this time I don't even know the name of it, won't until
I read about it later—just let it happen as it comes to my knowl-
edge that I don't know who he is but a strange man with whom
I'm entrapped in an office building in an unfamiliar city.

Where did I lay my purse after we came in? I can't remember. And what were the lock mechanisms on the doors like
and how quickly could I get through them?

But won't he get mad at me?

What will happen after?

Keep him happy and you'll be safer than if he's not, a voice apart
from but inside me says.

He leads me outside his office space.

We are small inside the vast space of the main floor the
ceiling goes up up and beneath it I am smaller more kissing
more jabbing into me his face leering at me he is—

Ugly. Skin stretched too tight across the sick, giddy, intoxicated face.

"Is this too rough?" he leans in to whisper in my ear as he
jabs at me.

The words are more than themselves: a challenge.

My only reply is to in the dimness hold his eyes.

"Get down on your hands and knees."

———————

Quiet, only the sound of their breath in the darkness. He holds her. They lay on their sides with her spooned into him, a sheet he apparently remembered to in advance have on hand (did he get it when they went back to the apartment?) over them. She is cold and in as much shock as relief because he seems tamed and settled, extinguished, and though the light of the morning doesn't yet touch the window she knows that it can't be very much longer, can it, till it comes?

The feeling that with the light she'll be safe and eventually free of him.

Is she asleep? he wants to know. He is oblivious that she's become a half person. He seems to assume she's the same person he knows (and doesn't know) from before.

May he masturbate over her? Is that okay?

Okay.

Then she sees what she thought might've been a distortion of her own damaged consciousness is real: something is wrong with his leg, or the skin of it. Patches of discoloration and a texture that seems too rough in one way and too smooth in another. It runs the length of one leg, into the groin area, and shows on part of the other upper leg. Something about his erect penis looks unnatural too. Something is different about it. Its thickness does not appear blood-swollen in that way she knows; there is something dense about it; the erection more rigid than it ought to be. The smooth parts of the skin of his leg have a plastic sheen. *Burned*, she understands.

Through a big picture window she sees the night-draped facade of the building across the street. All night the lamps to someone's living room have been on, but no one has entered it, and even if they had, it's far away enough that if they'd looked out, they probably wouldn't have noticed the couple across and above. Briefly they might've been able to see his long, naked white back as he stood over her masturbating, his semen gleaming in the half-light.

In what seems only a very short time later he is again erect, wanting her, wants her to put it in her mouth.

She sees in the dimness how its skin is more coarse and opaque than her husband's; no sign of a vein. She has no feelings about the act. He doesn't seem put off but rather turned on by the stunned-animal quality of her.

She thinks she should swallow but she feels she will choke; she spits; apologizes for fear of insulting him.

He wants to put his mouth between her legs. She lies there feeling his tongue work at her, the feeling as always like the sound of someone tapping from the other side of a glass pane. More pronounced than any sense of arousal is the occasional scratch of the bristle of his beard.

Why won't she come? What is it going to take? he wants to know. He is irritated.

She tells him she can't.

Oh. His pity. Disappointment. *It's okay. That's how some people are.*

Still. They lay in the dark a long time. Is he asleep?

But then:

"You're beautiful. You're so beautiful. You know, don't you? People treat you differently. My sister was beautiful. You get treated differently."

The wonder in his voice undercuts the envy: she finds it affirming, reassuring, maybe because it is so close to reverence, which carries with it the hint of a promise. *Safe now*, she thinks. *Saved*. The reverence passes into his hand, his fingers moving lightly from the caved-in space between her breasts to her navel, where a finger traces the curve of it. The touch is so light that sometimes the finger seems to be hovering. Then for some reason the fingers are at her neck, the lobe of her ear. Wonder. She can feel it in the touch. Radiating.

Into her hair he murmurs everything that comes to him. His family was poor but he went to an elite private school paid for by his grandfather. They lived on the bad side of town. Years ago he loved a woman whom he thought he'd marry but it didn't work. He walked out. He tried to get her back but she laughed at the idea of it. He liked another woman but that woman chose his best friend. He could make his sister laugh but it had never been easy. She said, "About forty percent of your jokes are funny and the other sixty percent are really bad." When she was ill, he got into the habit of before bed thinking of what he'd do to make her laugh the next morning. "The stakes got higher and higher," he said. "She was trying to not laugh unless it was really funny. She was trying to help me improve, she claimed. It was the service she was providing for me for my taking care of her as I was. She thought the strangest things were funny. Every morning I brought her tea and oatmeal, and one morning I paid a student to dress like me and bring it to her. This was a student who everyone said resembled me. People at the school had asked if we were related. She didn't see him come in. She just woke up to find a man who looked similar to me, dressed like me, with her breakfast. She started crying. I'd thought it

would be funny but when I appeared and she finally understood, she was furious. 'I worried I was losing my mind, you
asshole. How would you like it if you were dying of cancer and
someone was screwing with your head like that?' Hours later
she was laughing about it though. She laughed about it on
and off for days."

He is crying. "I'm not crying," he says. "It's my contacts."
With his finger he wipes away the drops.

Then: "Your eyes look like the eyes of this dog I wanted as
a kid." An Alaskan husky. He seems to think she should take
this as a compliment.

He is sorry for being annoyed with her for being late at the
gallery. He'd thought she wasn't coming. Once he waited for
two hours for his mother in a park in the middle of the day
in July. By the time he left sweat was pouring down his face.
His mother didn't call to explain. Later he found out his
mother had forgotten she was supposed to meet him. "That is
because she decided she didn't want to meet me," he explained.
"She didn't want to and so she forgot."

He tells her he used to paint too but he wasn't any good,
and that the mixing of colors disturbed him.

"Every time I mixed a color I liked I was afraid I could
never get that color back again," he says. "Do you ever worry
you can't mix the right color again?" he says to her.

"No," she replies. This seems rather ludicrous to her.
Though challenging at times, it certainly isn't that hard to mix
the right color; certainly not hard enough to merit fear of loss.
She's been coming a little back into herself as he holds her
and rambles on. Her sense of bafflement at him—at the way
his mind works, at him as an individual man rather than any
man, at someone becoming not a stranger—is strange enough

to through her increasing sense of curiosity nudge her into a more complex state of consciousness.

"I was in a house fire," he tells her. "Our living room caught on fire. It was like one of those stupid public-safety commercials they used to run—my mother fell asleep holding a cigarette. She feels so guilty about it she doesn't like being around me."

"Get on top of me," he said, and I did, as I'd have most likely done whatever he'd told me, as I had already, except for earlier in the night being able to come as he'd wanted.

It is almost over and it will never happen again, I thought, staring over at the gray wall across from me as I found the rhythm.

I can go home to my husband and figure out how to fix whatever is wrong with me that has led me into this bizarre situation.

"Look into my eyes," he said, trying to draw me away from the wall.

"Look," he said again, when I resisted. I had never looked into my husband's eyes during sex.

The sun was rising, the light flowing in through the windows.

I did as I was told.

"Now kiss me," he said.

"Eyes.

"Kiss me.

"Eyes.

"Kiss.

"Eyes."

A shiver went through me. Something was happening I couldn't understand; something stirring in my arms and legs.

He shuddered.

His eyes rolled back as he came.

He held me. I stayed quiet not because I was upset or scared anymore but because I no longer wanted to escape. His legs with their cool, hairless skin pressed into my legs. His arm curved over my waist; his hand reached for mine, laced our fingers. At the airport his musk would be all over me like the animal stares of strange men who sensed what had happened. The scent of us I would for hours breathe in by pressing my arm to my nose when no one was watching—a drug to dull the ache of the bruises ripening between my legs.

It would be six months before he ended it, when sitting across from me at a table at lunch he saw in my face watching his that I was in love with him.

"Are you asleep?"

He wanted me to claim him that morning. I could hear it in his voice.

"Why are you being so quiet? Are you all right?"

In my dreams he appeals to me still.

"*Hey*. Are you with me? Are you there?"

Please don't leave me.

That morning it seemed as if something monstrous and terrible—something until then looming over both of us—had been avoided.

"I'm here."

There is nowhere else to go now. The room fills with light.

ACKNOWLEDGMENTS

Thank you—

To my parents, Martin and Lavada, and to Jason, Terra, and Jonas, for their love and support during the writing of this book.

To Chad Lawson, for believing in me back in the days when I didn't much believe in myself.

To those whose companionship strengthened me at various times during the writing of this book: Suzanne Bodson, Wensi Chin, Elizabeth Mira, Nick Bazin, Joanna Stein, Amanda Stewart, Laura Dyar, Jillian Weise, Leighton Gleicher and Joe Feczko, Stephanie Snyder Benouis, Travis Scott, Jessica Alexander, Seth Rouser, Emilia Autenzio, and Dani Frid Rossi, and with special thanks to Sarah Gray for her steady, considerate, and loving presence these years.

To teachers, professors, and mentors who made me better and/or gave me encouragement at the right time: Scott Ely, Marjorie Sandor, Ann Pancake, David Huddle, Stan and Judith Kitchen, Adrianne Harun, Tom Barbash, Kevin Clark, Justin Cronin, Dr. John Bird, Dr. Steve Choate, Sherry Organ, Beverly Austin, Juanita Marrett, Bill Evans, Eva Esrum, Betty Fleming, Jeff and Cindy Payne, Emma Chandler, and Brian Delaney.

To Carl Lancaster, for his consistent kindness, wisdom, humility, faith, generosity, optimism, and trustworthiness.

To everyone who prayed for me when my life was not going so well.

For those who read parts of this manuscript and at critical times graced me with their constructive criticism, encouragement, and/or reading suggestions: Marjorie Sandor, Cameron Cottrell Walker, Ann Pancake, Chad Lawson, Donald Antrim, David Huddle, Rebecca Nagel, Sarah Gray, Amanda Stewart, Amie Barrodale, Adrianne Harun, Jamie Quatro, Karen Green, Scott McClanahan, Jillian Weise, James Yeh, C. Michael Curtis, Rivka Galchen, David Gordon, Blake Butler, Seth Rouser, Jonathan Franzen, Emily Cooke, and Louisa Thomas.

To the magazine and literary journal editors who've supported and published my work: Darren Pine; Garrett Doherty, Anthony Varallo and *Crazyhorse*; David Daley and *Five Chapters*; Amie Barrodale, Clancy Martin, Ryan Grim, and *VICE*; Jamie Quatro, Roger Hodge, Eliza Borne, and *Oxford American*; Laura Cogan, Oscar Villalon, and *ZYZZYVA*; and with special thanks to Lorin Stein and *The Paris Review* for their extraordinary promotion and support of my writing.

To the board of *The Paris Review* for honoring me with the Plimpton Prize for Fiction and for their generous support.

To the Corporation of Yaddo, for time and space and community, and to the Whiting Foundation who with Yaddo gave me much-needed financial assistance.

To the Rainier Writing Workshop faculty and students from 2004–2008.

To Mitzi Angel, formerly of FSG, for her faith, patience, love of my writing, and for the honor of her attention; to Emily Bell of FSG, for so warmly picking up where Mitzi left off and for being such wonderful hands for this book to fall into; to both Mitzi and Emily for their sharp vision and editorial brilliance; and to Maya Binyam and Brian Gittis and the FSG team for their support.

To Michael Shavit, formerly of *Granta*, for wanting this manuscript, and to Laura Barber of *Granta*, for her understanding of and enthusiasm for my writing and for this book.

To Andrew Wylie and the Wylie Agency, for their excellence; to Tracy Bohan of the Wylie Agency, for taking me on and believing in my writing and for her kindness; and to Rebecca Nagel of the Wylie Agency, for her compassionate and reassuring presence, for her understanding of and insight into my writing; and to Cecilia Kokoris for her support.

To Amie Barrodale, for offering me a hand when I was down in a hole.

And to Donald Antrim, for his love and spirit, and for wanting the best for me.

Keep in touch with
Granta Books:

Visit grantabooks.com to discover more.

GRANTA